WEDDING CEREMONY WOES

Steve Higgs

contents

NOT AGAIN

"*It stinks around here,*" complained Amber, licking her right front paw and using it to wash an ear. "*What fool thought to invite a pack of rabid mongrels to a wedding?*"

Lifting his head from the carpet to stare at the annoying Ragdoll cat, Buster the bulldog sniffed the air.

"*What are you talking about? It smells great here.*" He sniffed again, snorting in a huge, extended lungful to demonstrate how much he was enjoying it. "*Dogs, dogs, and more dogs.*"

"*Precisely,*" snapped Amber, placing her paw back down and eyeing her enforced companion critically. "*It's bad enough having to breathe in your stench all the time. The mixture of overlapping odours currently assailing my nostrils is too much.*"

Buster rolled onto his front. "*Well, for starters, moggy,*" he employed a term he knew she hated, "*you only think it's odd to invite dogs because no one would ever be crazy enough to do the same thing with cats. Dogs, as you know, are a man's best friend. Cats are a plague upon humanity, only surviving because nature granted them the gift of cuteness and because people are suckers for your saucer-sized eyes.*"

Amber made her eyes go huge to emphasise his point.

"*Secondly,*" Buster continued, "*there are no rabid mongrels here. This is the cream of canine society. There are no less than two Crufts group winners, several best in breed, and the groom's Doberman was second reserve for best in show last year.*"

Amber rolled her eyes. "*What utter tosh, Buster. They are nothing but preening narcissistic cretins too in love with themselves to understand how ridiculous they look as they prance around the arena.*"

Buster secretly agreed, but it didn't do to let the cat win points, so he shot back, "*Given that you are only mostly Ragdoll, and part goodness knows what else, you might not want to shout too loudly about pedigree status.*"

Amber's jaw dropped open, and she felt all eighteen claws extend.

"*Mostly Ragdoll?*" she growled. "*Mostly Ragdoll!*"

The cat and dog bickering is not a new thing, nor is the fact that I can hear them, but before I deal with it, I suppose I should give you at least a brief introduction.

My name is Felicity Philips. I'm fifty (mumbles) years old, short and petite with dark hair that is almost black, and I make my living as a wedding planner. A rather exclusive wedding planner actually. I cater mostly to the rich and pick up a lot of celebrity clients along the way.

Amber and Buster are my pets who, through an odd quirk of fate, I can understand. The noises they make appear in my head as fully formed words. Incessantly. Most days I find myself questioning whether it is a gift or a curse, but have to admit the unique connection I have to them has proven useful many times in the past.

Notably, both my cat and my dog have helped me to prove I was not guilty of murder, kept me alive when someone was trying to murder me, and have aided me in (sort of) solving a few crimes. I say sort of because the truth is I have never really solved anything. I just kind of stumble along trying to figure out who is behind whatever is going on, get it wrong, accuse a bunch of innocent people, and through dumb luck arrive at the truth in an unwitting manner.

Right now though, Amber and Buster were getting on my nerves.

"Oh, do stop arguing, you two," I felt myself forced to interrupt, pushing back from my dressing table. "There really is no need for it." Upon turning around to face my pets, I found they were glaring at each other with such intensity it would not have surprised me if laser beams began to shoot from their eyes.

With a sigh, I chose to do some parenting. "Buster, Amber is one hundred percent Ragdoll." Truthfully, I had no idea if that was true. Both Buster and Amber had come from a rehoming centre. She looked like a pedigree Ragdoll though, just as Buster appeared to be all bulldog and that was good enough for me. "Please apologise."

Buster, his eyes beginning to water as he refused to blink or look away from the cat, snapped his head around to check I was being serious.

"*What!*"

"*Yes,*" agreed Amber, returning to licking her paw and washing her ear. "*Apologise, you flea-bitten mutt.*"

"You too, Amber," I insisted. "You have no right to say that it stinks of dogs. I can't smell a thing."

Frowning, Amber pointed out, "*That's because you're a human and your nose doesn't work, Felicity.*"

"*She's got a point there,*" Buster found himself agreeing with the cat and quickly corrected himself. "*Which is not a polite thing to point out, Amber. How about if you apologise for that?*"

The bickering was about to descend into outright chaotic insults which would then often escalate into a chase around the room. However, on this occasion, the escalation was interrupted by an ear-splitting scream.

I froze, my feet rooting themselves to the spot as inside I groaned. I heard myself mutter, "Not again," before the adjoining door burst open and my assistant, Mindy, burst in.

"You heard that, right?" Mindy asked in an energetic, urgent tone.

Buster jumped to his paws. "*I did. Devil Dog reporting for duty. Sorry, forgot to do the voice.*" He lowered it an octave and employed a false raspiness that he believed made him sound dark, dangerous, and unpredictable to bad guys everywhere. "*Devil Dog reporting for duty.*"

I was already on my way to the door, but I fired a question at Mindy with a frown.

"Why aren't you dressed?"

Mindy's face made a confused expression as she looked down at her fully clad body and back up.

"Um, I am dressed, Auntie."

At the door, I grabbed the handle and spun around, putting a hand out, palm up, to halt Buster's run.

"Stay here," I commanded, leaving Buster's disappointed face behind when I slipped outside with my niece in tow. Outside I said, "You are not dressed for the wedding, Mindy. We need to start getting everything set up. The wedding is in six hours."

Not wanting to argue with me since I am her employer, Mindy nevertheless felt it necessary to point out, "Yes, Auntie, six hours. Between now and then, I expect to have to run around helping caterers, chase the flower arrangers to make sure they are set up, go in and out of the kitchens to oversee preparations, run up and down stairs to visit the rooms of the wedding party, attend to three dozen other tasks, and most likely mop your brow. I'm not saying I cannot do that in a fitted blouse, pencil skirt, and heels, but for the purpose of expediency, I would rather spend at least the first few hours racing around as I am."

She was making a valid point and I raised a hand in surrender. "Yes, Mindy, sorry. You're right. What you are wearing is entirely appropriate for the day you have ahead. I'm a little … "

"It's the day of the announcement," Mindy completed what I was about to say. "I know. You have a lot riding on the outcome. Do you really think it won't be you?"

I didn't like that I was that easy to read. My nineteen-year-old niece was right though. Whether it was arrogance on my part or overconfidence, I believed that it ought to be me. The subject in question was that of who would be appointed to plan, manage, and oversee the next royal wedding. Prince Marcus, youngest of the three princes, was due to marry Nora Morley, a commoner, in a love story the press was having a field day with.

A high-end wedding planner by profession with three decades of experience under my belt, I knew I was one of only two or possibly three people who would be considered for the job. It wasn't about money, it was the prestige that came with it. If I got the job, I would be able to write my own cheques and eliminate the need for an advertising budget for years to come.

In a positive mood, I wholeheartedly believed I was worrying about nothing, and my reputation combined with the supporters I had at every level of the industry would be enough to ensure there really wasn't anyone else being seriously considered. Everyone around me supported that belief even though I never once voiced it myself.

However, the pessimistic, negative voice inside my head questioned everything. It wasn't without just cause. My recent run of weddings were all public disasters. Not that any of them were my fault, or even anything to do with the planning. But murders, happy couples deciding to not go through with it, and bad publicity in general, were all combining to convince me that I had a highly visible black cloud hanging over my head.

I didn't get to answer my niece because we were nearing the bride's room and it was clearly the source of the scream, because even though the high-pitched shriek had died away, the ruckus that followed it was in full swing.

Mindy got to the door first, knocked smartly, waited two seconds, then stepped to the side as she opened the door to let me in.

Ernie

"**S**omeone has taken Ernie!" Donna, my bride-to-be, wailed at me the moment her eyes locked onto mine.

The bridal suite was filled with concerned faces, the bride's sister and her three best friends, her mother, her imminent mother-in-law, her father, who I still suspected to be involved in gangland activity – the man reeked of criminality, and a small entourage of other friends and lesser family members had all congregated.

I walked directly across the room, Mindy coming in behind me and closing the door. Approaching the bride, who looked terrible by the way, with tears streaming down her face and blotchy eyes from crying, I asked, "When did you last see him?"

I almost made the mistake of asking who Ernie was. It wasn't a name I was familiar with, and I make a point of learning the name of pretty much everyone on the guest list – it's the little things that set me apart from my competition. However, my brain caught up with me to deliver the answer – Ernie is the bride's little dog and the ring bearer for the ceremony.

The bride, Donna Moscovitch, gawped at me, her eyes disbelieving when she squealed, "He was tucked up in bed with me last night. When I woke up, he was gone!" She barely made it to the end of the sentence before her words turned into wailing.

Stepping in to block my path and take over from her sister, Donna's elder sibling, Denise, added, "Ernie is a prize-winning champion, best in breed, Pomeranian. It's very possible one of the other breeders attending this event has dognapped him."

Donna wailed even louder, "Ernnnieeeeee!"

With a frown that was firmly aimed at her eldest daughter, Mrs Moscovitch snapped, "Think about what you are saying, Denise! You are always creating a crisis where there is only a drama."

Looking hurt, Denise tried to argue, but her mother was no longer paying her any attention. I watched as Mrs Moscovitch wedged herself in next to the weeping bride, pushing Denise out of the way to effectively side-line her.

Denise almost fell over as she tried to get out of the way and, looking embarrassed, stepped away to merge into the background.

The wedding had a heavy focus on pedigree dogs, of which the bride was a big fan and through which she had met her groom. Many of their friends were also breeders and leading names at international dog shows. That one of them might have taken the bride's dog seemed unthinkable, but that didn't mean it hadn't happened.

"Is it possible that he just got out?" I suggested tentatively.

Donna wailed, "No."

Denise spoke up again, meeting my eyes with a frank expression. "The door was locked, and the windows were closed. Ernie could not get out, and to Donna's knowledge, no one came in at any point during the night."

I asked, "What can we do to help?" Every wedding throws up a unique curve ball that I am yet to encounter, even after the thousand plus weddings I have arranged and managed. This was no different and we would get through it.

I seriously doubted dognapping was behind Ernie's disappearance. More likely, another breeder wanted him to get jiggy with their lady dog and had chosen to sneakily let him out of Donna's room for precisely that purpose.

We would waste some time dutifully scouring the venue, but I genuinely expected Ernie to show up of his own accord. Worst case scenario we wouldn't find him in time for the ceremony and would need to swap in a new ring bearer – perhaps the groom's dog.

However, when I attempted to express my thoughts and assurances in soothing tones, Donna went nuts.

"I am not getting married without Ernie!" she screamed in my face. The bride was hysterical. She wasn't my first one of those, but she was the first to hit full melt down point because her dog had wandered off.

Donna was … I want to say reclining on an elegant chaise longue which is precisely what a bride ought to be doing, but it would be far more accurate to say that she had collapsed into it. Around her – sitting on the carpet to hold her hand and hanging over the back to touch her shoulder and give comfort, her closest friends and family members were crowding her.

She was, however, inconsolable and when she spoke her words were barely intelligible.

"He's never been away from me," Donna whined. "Not since he was eight weeks old when I got him from the breeders. He must be so terrified."

"Don't worry, sis," Denise attempted to comfort her younger sister. "We'll find him. The wedding planner will get all the hotel staff on it, won't you?" Denise shot me a look that dared me to refuse.

In response to Denise's words, Mrs Moscovitch huffed in an annoyed manner, but refrained from saying whatever thoughts were in her head.

Denise closed her mouth once more, her lips pressed thin as she stopped herself from reacting. There was some tension between the mother and the maid of honour that I had not detected before.

Despite her elder sister's words of comfort, Donna wailed again, "I'm not getting married without him." Then, in true bridezilla style, she screamed, "Why are you all standing around doing nothing! Get out there and look for him! Tell Damien to stop whatever he is doing and join the hunt too!"

"I'll do it," volunteered Denise, once again stepping in to look after her younger sibling's needs, but to my surprise Mrs Moscovitch flapped a dismissive hand at her.

"Don't make such a fuss, Denise. You're always making a fuss. I'll speak with Damien. You'll only get it wrong and bring him up to Donna's room – he's not supposed to see the bride before the ceremony."

Denise muttered something no one heard, and her mother challenged her on it instantly.

"What was that, dear? You're mumbling again."

Denise spoke clearly and calmly though the strained tension in her voice was unmistakable. "I didn't say anything, Mother."

Denise's boyfriend, Hudson, who I knew only from the guestlist – he was a recent addition, stood to one side of the room, failing to interact with anyone and looking thoroughly bored. He was ridiculously good looking, especially to be dating Donna's rather plain older sister, and when I turned my head to speak to Mindy, I found her to be staring at him, her expression transfixed.

"Close your mouth, Mindy," I murmured quietly.

She did so, her eyes never leaving the aftershave advert perfect man casually leaning against a wall on the opposite side of the room.

A few moments later we left the bridal suite and I paused in the corridor outside to gather my thoughts. I still needed to finish getting ready for the day and fully expected the missing dog to appear of his own accord. Nevertheless, the family expected me to organise the search for little Ernie, so I was going to call the hotel manager – a man I knew well after so many weddings at his hotel – and get his staff involved.

Mindy's thoughts were attuned elsewhere.

"The bride's sister seems awfully uppity for someone dating that unspeakably handsome hunk of a man."

"You liked him, did you?" I asked rhetorically.

"Auntie, I could cover him in caramel and eat him with a spoon. I might have to have a word with Denise about how she landed him because she is punching massively above her weight."

"You will do no such thing," I warned. The wedding guests were our clients and were not to be grilled on such matters.

Mindy shook her head despairingly. "I wasn't being serious, Auntie."

Just then the door to the bridal suite opened, the conversation inside spilling out as Mindy and I quickly fell silent – it had been poor form to discuss our clients outside their room and I prayed the people inside hadn't heard us.

Denise poked her head out, obviously looking for us. Closing the door quietly behind her in a manner that suggested she didn't want anyone to know she had left the room, she hurried over to where we were standing and spoke in a hushed tone.

"The police are on their way. I thought you would want to know."

"The police?" I questioned with a frown.

"Donna insisted they be called. She's convinced this is a dognapping and a ransom will follow."

I did nothing to hide my disbelief. "You're serious?"

The maid of honour's features darkened. "This *is* serious, Felicity."

Mindy stepped in. "Don't worry, Denise. Mrs Philips will get to the bottom of it." There she was volunteering my sleuthing services again even though I was rubbish at figuring these things out.

Denise relaxed a little and admitted, "Honestly, I think Donna is overreacting. Ernie probably did get out of her room and will be found chasing the bunnies in the garden."

That made me feel a bit better about questioning a client's judgement.

"I'd, ah ... I'd better get back inside," Denise made her excuse and quietly let herself back into the hotel's bridal suite.

Left alone again, and with the pressure of a busy day weighing me down, I chose not to hang around.

Walking beside me, Mindy asked, "Do you think her dog really could have been taken by someone, Auntie?"

Mindy's question hit the nail on the head. What did I believe? I sucked in a deep breath and weighed up my options. Releasing it slowly, I asked, "Did you see how nervous Mr Moscovitch looked?"

"No." Mindy's cheeks coloured. "I was too busy looking at Hudson."

"Well, he did." I thought back to previous conversations about Mr Moscovitch. He looked like a gangster. He looked like the type of person who cut off fingers one by one to get what he wanted. His head was like a bowling ball covered in skin, the few hair follicles still clinging to their jobs had their efforts shaved down to nothing. Tattoos crept out from the cuffs and collar of his perfect, crisp white shirt and he had teardrops beneath his right eye. He had to weigh two hundred and fifty pounds and was huge across his shoulders with bulky biceps and thighs straining the material of his Armani suit.

He was not someone I wanted to cross, and he rarely spoke. Adding together all the times I'd been in his presence I wouldn't need to take my shoes off to count the number of words I'd heard leave his lips.

What was with that?

Tapping into my inner sleuth, or trying to at least, I said, "If Ernie has been taken, I won't be surprised if it has to do with Mr Moscovitch's gang connections."

"Auntie," Mindy sniggered, "we don't know that he is a gang boss, or a henchman or whatever."

"Then where does his money come from?" I countered. "He's attended all his daughter's fittings, cake tastings, and other meetings, so he clearly doesn't have a regular job. I've never met anyone who looks more like a gangster. Have you?"

Mindy couldn't answer that one and I couldn't shift the feeling that I was right on the money. I was going to have to spy on Mr Moscovitch; I could feel it. The bride's little dog was missing, and it was barely nine in the morning. The sun was only just up, yet the day was going sideways despite my intricate planning.

If it wasn't a case of Ernie slipping out when no one noticed and there really was someone behind his disappearance, what did that mean? With that question playing on a loop inside my skull, I hurried back to my room.

ON THE RUN

In a different wing of the hotel and far from the drama unfolding in Donna Moscovitch's life, Albert Smith, a man nearing his eighties and inexplicably on the run from the law despite a career as a police detective that spanned several decades, was thinking about breakfast.

His dog, an oversized German Shepherd and former police dog called Rex Harrison, was thinking very much along the same lines.

The question, so far as Albert saw it, was whether to risk going to the restaurant for breakfast or play it safe and have them bring it to his room. It was not an equation Albert found easy to balance.

The likelihood of being spotted by anyone who might recognise him was slim – it wasn't as if his face graced wanted posters across the nation. Also, if they brought his cooked breakfast to the room, Albert was willing to bet it would be cold, or lukewarm at best, by the time he started to eat it.

Whichever solution he chose, he was going to eat, pack his things, and move on. Crashing at the hotel last night was only to ensure he wasn't staying at his house where the police were very possibly going to look for him. That he was wanted at all was ridiculous, so allowing them to take him into custody and then question him might be the shortest solution to clearing his name.

That eventuality wasn't guaranteed though, and the senior officer pursuing his arrest wasn't known for listening to reason. No, the best and only way out of his dilemma was to catch the man behind the recent death and destruction with which Albert's name had been aligned.

Albert would vacate the hotel soon, heading west toward Cornwall and covering his movements because the police would be monitoring his bank and credit cards. Too savvy to get caught so easily, Albert was glad to have friends upon whom he could rely.

Breakfast though - he didn't want to leave without breakfast and the smell of bacon was already in his nostrils.

He'd risked taking Rex for a walk already, getting out early when there was almost no one around to see him. Was his face on the news? Albert doubted it, but playing it safe was the right strategy.

"I'm going to get breakfast," Albert announced, putting down his book and heading for the door.

Rex bounced onto his paws, his tail wagging as he trotted swiftly after his human.

"Great idea. I can taste the bacon already."

Albert gripped the door handle with his left hand and used his right to block Rex's path.

"No, boy, you stay here."

Rex couldn't believe his ears. *"But we always have breakfast together."*

Unlike the wedding planner, Albert had no ability to understand what his dog was saying and had to figure out what the dog wanted or what he was thinking from his expressions and body movement. This one was easy to interpret.

"Sorry, Rex. Not this time. If the police have circulated a description, they will be looking for an old man with a large German Shepherd dog. We need to minimise how much we expose ourselves this close to home. It won't be so bad once we get out of the county." Albert ruffled the thick fur on Rex's head and slipped out the door.

Finding the restaurant was a task he'd undertaken last night. As part of his plan to remain unnoticed, he had avoided the bar, eaten dinner in his room with food from his backpack, and was studiously avoiding speaking to members of hotel staff unless it was absolutely necessary.

Going for breakfast broke those rules, but he was hungry and willing to risk it, for what is life without a full English?

Hiding behind a complimentary broadsheet newspaper, Albert sipped his tea and waited for his freshy cooked plate of goodies to arrive.

DEVIL DOG TIME!

Turning left when I reached the end of the corridor, I passed a window and screeched to a halt at what I saw outside. There were police cars, a stream of them, barrelling down the tree-lined driveway leading to the hotel.

Were they here because of Ernie?

I counted three cars plus a van, and their speed of approach showed an urgency I didn't believe the situation demanded.

Pushing it from my mind and cancelling my plan to get the hotel staff involved in the search – if the police were getting involved, the dog would be found swiftly or wasn't here to be found at all – I took out my phone and dialled my master of ceremonies.

"Good morning, Felicity." Justin's jovial tones were most welcome. "I'm just coming along the bypass. I'll be with you in five minutes."

That was good news. Justin has a young family and doesn't stay away overnight unless he has to. With this wedding being so close to home, you might question why I had chosen to stay there and the answer is I learned long ago that being at the venue the night before tackles a lot of potential dramas. Also, one time there was a crash on the motorway, and it took me four hours to get to the wedding. I was never going to let that happen again.

"Just so you know, the police are here." I got nothing but silence from the other end. "Justin?"

"Still here," he replied. "I was waiting for you to tell me who has been murdered."

"No one, thankfully." I sure hoped that remained true. My recent run of crazy wedding debacles were getting me down. "The bride's dog has gone missing. It's probably nothing," I added. "Though Donna believes he's been dognapped and that's why the police are here."

"The police?" Justin questioned. "For a missing dog?"

I nodded even though he couldn't see the gesture. "Yes. It is rather strange."

We were walking through the hotel en route back to my room. I was going to finish getting ready, but it had occurred to me in the last few seconds, that Buster might be able to use his nose to find Ernie. Mindy could walk him around to see the wedding guests staying at the hotel, and pretending to check they were aware of the timings for the ceremony and knew where to congregate, she could have my bulldog sniff around.

It was simple, it was genius, and if we found and returned Ernie the minor drama would be squared neatly away just like my advertising claimed.

Justin cleared the line and I put my phone away. I would meet him at the hotel lobby in just a few minutes and there we would divide up some of the tasks Mindy would no longer be able to tackle. There is always a lot to do on the day of the wedding, the list Mindy recited earlier a fairly accurate reflection of how many tasks could not be started until a few hours before the ceremony.

"Are we going back to your room?" Mindy asked when I walked past the top of the stairs - she'd expected to head down them.

I didn't get to answer Mindy because Philippe, my other assistant, arrived in the corridor ahead of us with his usual over the top exuberance and flamboyance.

Under her breath, Mindy said, "Wow."

Philippe is a makeup artist who quit his job after sleeping with his boss, and through ill-timing on my part, ended up working for me. I'm not complaining ... exactly. It's just that I have an image. The business has an image. We are high-end catering to celebrities and the very rich. It's a niche market and my earlier moaning to Mindy about her choice of sportswear was all to do with my desire to make sure the image we presented could only be described as impeccably polished.

Philippe was impeccably dressed for sure, but the pink zebra-print three-piece suit with matching top hat and chrome-topped swagger stick were not quite what I had in mind.

"I just came from your room," he announced. "You're not there."

Mindy sniggered at him. "Really, Philippe? Aren't we?" My two assistants got on really well with each other; a friendship blooming, and I silently questioned whether Mindy had been drawn into what seemed to be a fashion for finding a gay BFF.

Philippe made a cat hissing noise and mock swiped the air at Mindy, his hand pretending to be a cat's paw.

I hurried past him. "We are going there now, Philippe, however I need you to head down to the kitchens and liaise with Chef O'Malley. You have your tablet with you?" I queried, pausing to check he did since I couldn't see it.

On cue, Philippe whipped his electronic device from the over the shoulder man bag he wore.

"Jolly good. Listed in catering under the Moscovitch wedding, you will find a master register of all the food being delivered for the wedding. A few items, the non-perishables, arrived yesterday and I saw them unloading more items a short while ago. You can see what has been checked off. Please liaise with which ever one of her assistants Chef O'Malley has assigned to the task and let me know what is still to be delivered."

It was commonplace for there to be something that didn't arrive as expected, even though I used the most reliable caterers in the business. If that proved to be the case, I wanted to be able to chase it sooner rather than later.

I got an, "Aye, aye," from Philippe and he scurried away to get on with his first task of the day.

Once he was out of earshot, I asked Mindy, "Where does he get his outfits from?"

Mindy saw fit to snigger again; she thought his choice of clothing was entertaining, but revealed, "He's got a friend who makes them for him." It sounded more plausible to me than a shop was out there selling such items off the peg.

Arriving outside my room, I could hear Buster snuffling at the gap under the door.

Swiping my card against the lock, I called out, "Back up, Buster, we are coming in."

My excitable bulldog had done as instructed, however backing up, so far as Buster was concerned, meant moving about three feet.

He was jumping up at me in his usual daft manner before I could get into the room and his questions came in a torrent. *"What was that scream that we heard?"* he wanted to know. *"Do we have a murder? Is there a case to investigate? Is it Devil Dog time now?"*

Amber, looking for all intents and purposes as though she were asleep in a sunny spot on the windowsill, muttered, *"Stupid dog."*

To answer Buster's questions, I said, "There has not been a murder, but the scream you heard was from the bride. Her Pomeranian has gone missing."

"Ernie?" Buster sought to confirm.

"Indeed. So yes, it is, in fact, time for Devil Dog to make an appearance. I need you to go with Mindy and see if you can sniff him out?" I think Buster would have saluted if his limbs would perform such a complicated motion. Instead, his chest visibly swelled and I saw him looking into the middle distance with a strange expression on his face.

"Is he attempting to smoulder?" asked Mindy.

My niece is aware of my unique ability to communicate with Amber and Buster. Like everyone else on the planet, she only hears the animal noises they make, but she has grown used to figuring out what is being said from my half of the conversation.

I nodded. "Yes, Mindy, I believe that is precisely what he is doing."

"Shall I get straight on with that then, Auntie?"

Buster stopped smouldering to dance around energetically by her feet, a continuous happy chant coming from him. *"It's Devil Dog time. It's Devil Dog time. The time is nigh for the bad guys to feel the justice of Devil Dog."*

"It's just a missing Pomeranian," I pointed out to him. "There is no reason yet to believe that anything untoward has taken place."

Mindy pulled a face. "I don't know, Auntie. The bride seemed quite convinced that Ernie has been dognapped."

Amber snorted in amusement but offered no comment.

Buster looked up at me his eyes narrowed. *"Dognappers, eh? Well, I'll fix their wagon,"* he drawled in a terrible John Wayne impression.

"The police are here," I reminded my niece. "If someone has taken Ernie, I'm sure they will deal with it. Sending you out is just a precaution."

"Maybe there'll be a ransom note," chortled Amber from the windowsill. Her eyes were still closed, but the humour of the situation was getting the better of her and she was laughing more and more. Her eyes opening wide, she swung her head to look at me when she spluttered, *"One million gravy bones or the fluffball gets it!"*

I frowned at her. "You are being unkind again, Amber."

"What are you talking about?" questioned Buster. *"She's never anything other than unkind."*

Amber narrowed her eyes at the bulldog, a sneer crossing her face, so before the two could start fighting again I sent Mindy on her way.

With Buster's lead in her hand, and the dog attempting to drag her down the corridor, Mindy held onto the door frame to ask a last question.

"What do we do if he cannot be found?"

DISAPPOINTINGLY FAMILIAR FACES

I continued pondering Mindy's question all the way down to the lobby to meet Justin. Assigning my niece to have Buster find and track the Pomeranian's scent was almost certainly unnecessary, yet something in my head insisted I might regret not doing something proactive. The bride was refusing to get married without her dog in attendance and the clock was ticking: less than six hours until the ceremony was due to start. With so much to do today, I could not afford to spend any more time wondering what might have happened to Ernie.

Possibly, it was the impending decision regarding the royal wedding that was making me so blasé about his disappearance. It wasn't that I didn't care; I was truly concerned for the little chap's wellbeing.

However, I wasn't convinced there was anything more I could do for him that wasn't already being done.

The police were here, after all – enough of them to sweep through the hotel and I imagined they would deputise, or whatever the right word was, a bunch of the hotel staff to assist them.

Unfortunately, it turned out that I was dead wrong about the police

Arriving at the foot of the sweeping, grand staircase with the hotel's lobby and guest reception area spread out ahead of me, I could not only see a gaggle of uniformed police officers heading my way, but could also hear them.

More accurately I could hear one of them and it brought me no pleasure to recognise his voice.

"Of all the ridiculous nonsense. They are lucky I'm not charging them all with wasting police time," raged Chief Inspector Ian Quinn. He was walking fast, his strides fuelled by visible righteous anger. That he was leaving did not need to be explained, and I paused where I was rather than continue onwards and risk him spotting me.

However, luck or fate, whichever you wish to ascribe to, chose to deal me a different hand.

"Felicity," hallooed Justin, waving enthusiastically as he came through the hotel's front doors. It was enough to make the chief inspector twitch his eyes in my direction and the sight of me was enough to make his feet grind to a halt.

He stopped moving so quickly the officers following in his wake all piled into one another as the closest did everything he could to not mow down his now stationary boss.

That Chief Inspector Quinn did not like me was well established. We first met a couple of months ago at a wedding that went spectacularly sideways. There were several murders which he was assigned to solve and was most put out when my old friend Patricia Fisher figured it all out before he could tie his shoelaces.

I'd been forced to endure his company since then as unfortunate circumstances threw us together and most recently had cause to slap his face. Had my assault not been justified, and witnessed by other officers who I believed would back up my claim, I'm quite certain he would have pressed charges.

Wheeling around to face me, Chief Inspector Quinn slowly and very deliberately placed a fist on each of his hips.

"Why am I not surprised to see you here, Mrs Philips? Your idea, was it? Tell the police a three-year-old has gone missing in suspicious circumstances and have us all scrambling to react as such a situation demands only to discover that a rather pertinent fact has been omitted from the details. The three-year-old isn't a child at all, it's a damned dog!"

Returning his glare and refusing to be cowed, I said, "I can assure you, Chief Inspector, that I had nothing to do with any call placed to the police or anyone else regarding the matter of the missing champion

Pomeranian and was surprised to see police cars arriving. I take it that you are not going to be investigating?"

My question drew a snort of disbelief, the Chief Inspector mugging away to look at his subordinates as he questioned if I was being serious. His officers, men and women in uniform with the exception of one, reacted in an obediently amused manner as he clearly expected them to. The one who didn't was at least twenty years older than the others and in plain clothes - a detective. Looking to be in his mid-fifties, he wasn't willing to pretend that he was entertained by the chief inspector's antics. Instead, he was studying me, a hand cupping his chin as thoughtful eyes burned into mine.

We knew each other, of course, and that was why he was staring at me. I'd first met Detective Sergeant Mike Atwell when I attempted to sneak into the hospital room of an old friend. I was wanted for murder at the time and suspected of inflicting the injuries that landed my friend in the hospital. Obviously, I was completely innocent on both counts. DS Atwell could have just arrested me on the spot that day, but chose instead to let me explain. The truth came out shortly after but I had never really gotten around to thanking him.

I could have waved to him, but that would have singled him out. Before I could decide what to do, my attention was drawn back to Chief Inspector Quinn who was talking once again.

"I was going to leave this, Mrs Philips. However, I rather suspect you are lying about having a hand in the wasted police time, effort, and resources you see before you, so I shall investigate. If you were in any way involved, it would be best if you confessed now, thus avoiding any further wasted effort on my part." He stopped talking, letting the silence encourage me to speak. When, after several seconds, my lips were yet to move, he twisted to face his officers. "Grace, take Snoxell and go back to the bridal suite. I want statements from everyone including the bride. I want to know whose idea it was to call us."

I wanted to snap a response at the ignorant, arrogant, rude, self-important git, but he spun away from me, smartly twisting on his heels to once again stride at pace from the hotel.

His officers followed, even DS Atwell, though he paused by the door to give me one last thoughtful look before pushing his way through to vanish outside.

"Goodness, was that Chief Inspector Quinn," asked Justin, hurrying across the lobby to air kiss my cheek. Justin and I had worked side by side for many years, and he knew about my problem with the chief inspector. This was, however, the first time he had ever witnessed it for himself.

I nodded, not wanting to discuss the subject; I had too many other topics Justin and I needed to go over. It was another big wedding day. Three hundred guests in attendance, a lot of money being spent very fast, and a long sequence of things that I needed to stay on top of.

To be fair, Justin is the one who manages most of them on the day. I like to think of myself as a general preparing the troops for battle and giving them every chance of emerging victorious because of the strategies I have put in place. And like a general, when the bulk of the fighting occurred, I would be a mile behind the frontline, observing the battle and reacting to send reinforcements where they were necessary. Such a strategy is not possible if one is engaged in hand-to-hand fighting.

Don't ask me where the general analogy came from, it's just one I picked up somewhere over the years and it seemed to fit.

Justin was dressed and ready for the day in an elegant caramel suit from a leading London tailor - we get great discounts by sending work their way - and from his left hand hung a suit carrier in which his master of ceremonies outfit was concealed.

The first thing I intended to do with Justin was go through all the things that were yet to be checked off the list and show him around the enormous marquee in the garden. The marquee, freshly erected yesterday and still being decorated, would act as chapel and reception venue for the wedding. Before that, and because the police were not getting involved as I had hoped, I absolutely had to make sure the hotel staff was aware of the missing dog.

I took one pace toward the concierge desk and that was as far as I got.

"Mrs Philips!" yelled Phillipe, running into the lobby with a panicked look upon his face.

CAUGHT

The unexpected arrival of the police shocked Albert; an instant and unwelcome jolt of adrenaline filling his body. His heart began to race which was also quite unwelcome. No stranger to the sensation of his body preparing for fight or flight, Albert nevertheless felt unusually discombobulated this time.

He believed his careful actions had left no trail for them to follow, so it could only be that someone had spotted him and reported it.

When the line of speeding police vehicles caught his eye through the dining room window, Albert had just been mopping up the last of his egg yolk with a final piece of toast. Intending to be out of the hotel and on his way in the next thirty minutes, he now questioned how many minutes it might be before they placed him under arrest.

Four police cars felt like absolute overkill. It wasn't as if he could be considered dangerous. Or could he? Albert found himself questioning whether the stance the police were taking might be the right one given the circumstances. Chief Inspector Quinn's concerns, foolish and exaggerated though Albert knew them to be, were based upon Albert's knowledge of the presence of explosives in the seaside town of Whitstable.

For no good reason other than he knew nobody else was going to do it, Albert was investigating what he believed to be a master criminal at work. Unintentionally, during a culinary tour around the British Isles, Albert stumbled upon a long string of strange crimes involving the theft of specific food items and equipment for making food, and the kidnapping of chefs, bakers, and other experts from the food industry. No, that last part was wrong, Albert corrected himself. People had been going missing, but there was very little evidence of kidnap, and what evidence there was had only been witnessed by him.

The crimes had been occurring all over the country and it was only when viewed holistically and with a willingness to believe in the concept of there being a master criminal behind it all that any sort of link could be found between them.

Albert had found that link and knew with unshakeable certainty that he was right. A friend he'd made in Arbroath had gone missing and Albert was convinced it was at the hands of the very same master criminal, a person he dubbed as the Gastrothief. In large part, his hunt for the master criminal was all about finding that friend.

The police, with the exception of his children, were not taking the situation seriously, and his kids, all three of them senior detectives within the metropolitan police, were in hot water for using police resources to aid their father's private investigation.

Concern for his children's careers was another thing driving him to solve the case, for only in doing so could he unequivocally prove that his kids had been right to support him.

Now though, it looked as though he was caught. He folded his newspaper and set it to one side then drained the last of his tea and made use of the little time he believed he had left to return to his room.

He wasn't going to run, he was too old for such nonsense, and it would just make him look even more guilty. Leaving the dining room, Albert wasn't returning to his room to collect his bags, but to make sure Rex was with him when the police officers came. He needed to make sure his dog was taken care of correctly. Otherwise, he could imagine Chief Inspector Quinn sending Rex to the pound out of spite.

Walking calmly and with dignity, Albert made his way back through the hotel, however he didn't get to his room. There were two uniformed officers ahead of him when he stepped out of the elevator – they had obviously taken the stairs, and the sight made him freeze. He couldn't know it, but the police were on their way to the bridal suite which just happened to be a few doors along from Albert's room.

Seeking accommodation at the very last moment, Albert got one of the last rooms in the hotel, which was almost completely booked out for the wedding. The suite he was stuck in was vastly overpriced compared to the bed and breakfasts he more commonly frequented, however beggars cannot be choosers and he'd accepted the cost without comment.

Ducking back out of sight, Albert gritted his teeth and argued with himself about what to do next. Electing to not run away was one thing, but when they took him, it was going to be on his terms. He didn't see where they went, but when he peered around the corner again the two police officers were no longer in sight.

Assuming they were now in his room, Albert chose to retreat to the library. From there he knew he would have a view down over the lobby and would see if the police officers came out with Rex. Had it been anyone else coming into the room, Rex would have filled the world with his barking aggression, yet he always acted differently around police officers, a fact which Albert put down to his training.

Albert wasn't going to delay for very long, but knowing he was going to be taken into custody, he wanted to make several phone calls.

Quietly, and unnoticed by anyone, he slipped away.

cerberus

Buster was thoroughly enjoying his morning. He liked Mindy; she was fun to be around. Not that he disliked Felicity, of course, but Felicity never wanted to run anywhere, and Mindy loved to run.

They had visited sixteen rooms already, and had a whole bunch left to go if he correctly understood what Mindy was telling him.

A lot of the rooms had dogs inside; over half of them in fact, and at each one Buster was either having a jolly good sniff to confirm Ernie was not there and never had been or was having a swift conversation with the dog or dogs who were there to confirm they knew nothing about Ernie's mysterious disappearance.

When they left each room behind, Mindy would gamely run with him to the next one. He was generally out of breath whenever they arrived anywhere, but he didn't mind that so much and some of the rooms were next to each other.

Racing along one corridor, Buster's nose picked up a scent that caused him to dig his claws into the carpet.

"Ernie!" he barked at Mindy. *"I can smell Ernie! Ernie is here!"*

Mindy's arm almost left its socket when the squat, heavy dog chose to unexpectedly brake, and now Buster was barking at her.

"This is why it would be better if Aunt Felicity was with you," she observed, rubbing some life back into her shoulder with the opposite hand. "She would know what you were saying."

Buster tried again, this time speaking slowly as if to an imbecile. *"Ernie. is. here."*

Mindy put her hands on her knees and bent at the waist to bring her head down. Staring directly at Buster, she decided to try something.

"Now I can't understand you, Buster, but maybe you can respond to my questions. Are you trying to tell me you can smell something?" she asked and got an excited woof in return. "Can you smell Ernie the missing Pomeranian?" she guessed. When this time Buster leapt up on his back legs and tried to lick her chin, she asked, "We've just drawn level with the room he was staying in," she pointed to a door that said 'Bridal Suite' on it in ornate letters. "Are you smelling where he is, or where he has been?"

From behind the door to the bridal suite, Donna's voice screeched, "Get out! You're not supposed to see me before the ceremony. Daddy, tell him to get out!"

Buster's tail stopped wagging, and it did so just as the door to the bridal suite opened. Now able to get a better sniff, Buster shoved his head through the door.

Mindy let him do it, her attention on the person now filling the doorway. It was the groom, and he was looking rather embarrassed.

Trying to look without being obvious about it, Mindy noted that there were two police officers in the bridal suite and wondered where the rest of them had gone – she'd seen the number of squad cars speeding down the hotel's driveway, but wasn't about to ask.

Donna screeched again, "Do something useful, Damien, get Cerberus to sniff out where Ernie is."

Forcing Buster to back up again, a statuesque looking Doberman strode boldly through the door. The collar around his neck, which looked like rows of dark crystals, was attached by a lead to the groom's hand.

"*Step back, little dog,*" commanded Cerberus without even bothering to look down at Buster.

Buster blinked twice before he got his brain up to speed and by then the groom was in the corridor with Mindy and the bridal suite door was closing.

"*You're the Crufts second reserve,*" he gushed.

"*That's right. I am. Now step back and stop staring at me or I shall be forced to charge for basking in my magnificence.*"

The comment went straight over Buster's head, and he asked, *"Did I just hear that you are going to help look for Ernie? That's what I am doing."*

The Doberman looked down at the bulldog for the first time, one eyebrow cocked as he observed the lesser breed.

"What do you mean? Why would you be trying to find Ernie?"

Buster's keen expression fell, replaced by one of confusion.

"Because he's lost. Or no one seems to know where he is, at least. Do you want to team up?"

Cerberus was used to getting a certain amount of hero worship and in other circumstances might have been kind to the scruffy, slobbering idiot now scratching his ear with a back leg. However, he had his own plan for the day and it did not involve finding the Pomeranian.

"Pah!" he spat. *"That ridiculous little toy dog can stay lost for all I care. What kind of a dog is a Pomeranian anyway?"*

Buster couldn't stop his frown from forming.

"A dog is a dog, surely?" The Doberman was trying to challenge what Buster felt was a universal rule. Dogs were united in their diversity, not divided by it.

The Doberman's top lip twitched, an unspoken threat that his word should not be challenged. He was the top dog and everyone else needed to get in line.

"Be careful, little dog," he growled.

The groom twitched the lead in his hands. "Cerberus, behave."

Cerberus ignored the command. Glaring at Buster, he said, "Abandon this foolish quest to find Ernie. He will not be missed and will soon be forgotten. My human's mate will soon realise how wasted were her affections on such a silly dog when she could have been adoring me instead. I will act as ring bearer today."

The awe Buster had felt upon first meeting the Doberman just a few moments ago had completely evaporated. His stomach felt swirly, and he knew why: Cerberus was the bad guy. For a superhero to truly rise, he needed a worthy adversary and Devil Dog's was standing right in front of his face.

With his chest swelling and an imaginary cape flapping in a non-existent breeze, Buster growled, *"I don't know anything about bearing rings, but take heed, Cerberus, I mean to find the missing Pomeranian, and toy dog or not, I'm going to deliver him back to the bride and there's nothing you can do to stop me."* He leaned into his collar and showed the Doberman his teeth. "I'm basically a superhero," he boasted, *"and if you or anyone else get in my way, they will rue the day they were born."*

Cerberus wasn't used to being spoken down to by anyone, let alone a chunky bulldog with a dubious pedigree.

Mindy tightened her grip on Buster's lead and dragged him back a yard as the growls he and the Doberman were exchanging ratcheted up a notch in volume.

"Sorry about him," Mindy apologised to the groom. "He's not usually like this." Cutting her head and eyes down to look at Buster in time with giving his lead a jerk, she hissed "Pack it in, Buster."

"*He started it*," Buster whined, settling on the carpet to silently glare at the Doberman, "*and I think he might be the supervillain of this story.*"

Returning her attention to the groom, Mindy asked, "No luck finding Ernie then?"

Damien shook his head. "Sorry, no, not yet."

An awkward silence followed, Mindy and Damien each waiting for the other to say something.

When it became uncomfortable, Mindy pointed along the corridor in the direction she wanted to go, and said, "I'd, ah, I'd better be getting along. There's a lot to do today," she smiled at the groom, "someone's getting married."

Keeping a tight hold on Buster's lead, Mindy led him around the Doberman and set off once again, walking this time, not running, and it was because of that that Buster picked up another scent that made him dig in his claws.

Rex

Rex was bored. He was also hungry, but that was just because he'd imagined getting a plate to lick clean at breakfast and had been denied. His breakfast kibble was filling his belly quite adequately, though it was hardly the same thing as a piece of bacon or some leftover fried eggs.

A short while ago, he'd been listening for his human to return when he heard a squelch of radio coming his way. He needed the advance warning so he could jump off the bed and quickly tug the top cover with his teeth. He'd discovered that if he did that, it removed the indentation his body would leave, and his human would never know he'd been on it.

The radio noise was a very familiar sound from a previous career as a police dog. His life with Albert was better in many ways, but there had been more to do as a member of the Metropolitan Police Dog Service.

Sniffing to confirm what he already believed, his nose identified the combination of boot polish, starched clothing, and the very bass tang of steel combined with the oil police officers use to maintain the mechanism on their handcuffs.

Curious, Rex had hopped off the bed and padded over to the door. Two sets of footsteps went by, the leather scent and the creaking noise that went with it matching that recorded in his memory.

A few seconds later, Rex heard a knock, a few muffled words being exchanged, and a door closing to leave the corridor outside his room once again devoid of life.

That was ten minutes ago.

His human had been absent for a long enough time that Rex believed he ought to be returning quite soon. The old man had been talking about getting back on the road today; they were heading for somewhere called Cornwall apparently. Place names meant nothing to Rex, but he knew he would be able to tell if he'd ever been there before or not from the scents in the air when he arrived.

One of the best things about life with his human was how much travelling they did. They were always arriving somewhere new, and each location had its own set of smells to explore.

Wanting to return to the bed, yet believing he didn't have enough time to make it worthwhile, Rex was still lying on the carpet with his nose up against the gap under the door when he heard someone else coming.

Then he caught the scent of the bulldog he met a few hours ago in the grounds outside the hotel. He dredged his brain for a name.

"*Rex!*" the bulldog barked through the door. "*It's Devil Dog!*"

Ah, yes, Rex remembered the bulldog's strange obsession with having a superhero name.

"*Hello,*" he replied for something to say.

"*There's a missing Pomeranian,*" the bulldog explained through the door. "*If you see or smell it, let me know.*"

Rex heard a human speaking, the voice that of a young woman.

"Is Ernie in there?" the young woman asked. "Is that what you're trying to tell me?"

Rex heard the bewildered confusion in the bulldog's voice when he replied, "*No. Humans are so strange.*" Then speaking through the door once again the bulldog said, "*I've got to go. There's a dognapping case to solve and a Doberman to thwart.*"

Rex had no idea who the Doberman the bulldog referred to might be; he hadn't met one in the short time he been at the hotel, however the suggestion that there was a missing dog case to solve was thoroughly interesting.

Investigating what might have happened and putting his nose to good use, would chase away the boredom of sitting in his human's hotel room. If only he could open the door.

He was still pondering the problem ten minutes later when someone knocked on the door and called out, "Housekeeping."

Rex had been listening to someone appearing periodically in the corridor for most of an hour. The person, who smelled distinctly like cleaning products, would knock, utter a single word and then go quiet for the next fifteen minutes.

Backing away from the door, curious about what was going to happen next, Rex was delighted when the door suddenly opened inward. Recognising an opportunity when it presented itself, Rex lunged for the gap.

The lady from housekeeping was fiddling with her phone, paying little attention to her surroundings while organising drinks out with some of her girl pals the following Friday night. When her brain registered movement from the corner of her eye, it sparked a fear reaction that generated a scream as she threw herself away from what her base instincts perceived to be a mortal danger.

Rex shot past her legs, turned hard right, and set off to find the bulldog.

CRIMINAL BEHAVIOUR

"How quickly can you replace it, Felicity?" Chef O'Malley wanted to know. "I do not have a lot of time left and we still have a lot to do."

I was in the hotel's kitchen with Justin and Philippe beside me as all three of us inspected the food laid out on a stainless-steel counter.

The subject being discussed was the one hundred and fifty pounds of prime beef fillet and the three hundred fresh lobsters that had all been stained with blue ink. That neither product, the centre dishes for the wedding breakfast, were edible was thoroughly obvious.

"How did this happen?" I found myself asking. "Where were they?"

Chef O'Malley muttered something unrepeatable under her breath and walked across the kitchen to a pair of centre-opening doors. Designed for wheeling in centrepiece cakes or the like that wouldn't fit through a single door, Chef pushed the left side open and led us outside.

There she nodded her head toward a large white box measuring roughly fifteen feet by thirty.

"In the chiller," she huffed, unable to hide her irritation. "The beef came in yesterday, the lobsters this morning, just a couple of hours ago. I shouldn't have to place a guard on the refrigerator to prevent this sort of thing happening."

I didn't disagree, but just as I was thinking about the steps I needed to take next, I spotted Mr Moscovitch. He was all the way across the carpark, fiddling around with something in the boot of his car. The vehicle, a large German SUV, was facing me, the boot lid doing a good job of hiding what Mr Moscovitch was up to.

I watched, unable to take my eyes off the tattooed, muscular man when he turned to speak to someone. From the left, another man was approaching. He also wore a suit and though I couldn't see any tattoos on him, he was almost as physically imposing as Donna's dad.

The new man stopped behind the car parked next to Mr Moscovitch's. Using a key fob, he opened the car, its lights flashing once, and then raised the boot lid to access the rear load compartment.

Now my view of the two men was almost completely obscured, and I shifted position to get a better look.

"Felicity?" Justin questioned what I was doing.

I flapped a hand at him, begging a few seconds' grace. Mr Moscovitch was up to something – conducting secret business with one of his criminal colleagues or employees was what it looked like. Hidden from sight by the cars, my eyes popped from my head when I saw the man I didn't know hold up something long, thin and dark. I couldn't get a good enough angle to confirm what it was, but when he passed it to Mr Moscovitch, it had to move through the gap between the cars.

And I saw it clearly.

Only fleetingly, but my heart chose to stop beating for a moment anyway.

With my breaths coming in savage, shocked, gasps, I spun around to check the others had seen it too. They were all too busy discussing the food and what they were going to do about it.

"You saw that, right?" I gasped, getting three sets of eyes to swing my way.

"Saw what?" asked Chef.

Justin eyed me sceptically. "Are you all right, Felicity?"

"You didn't see it?" I squeaked, a hand to my chest as I started to feel a little faint.

"Whoa!" Justin came to my side, gripping my arm. "Let's get you inside and sitting down, shall we? Philippe, fetch a glass of water, please."

I needed a minute – my head had gone quite swimmy, but once I felt able to raise it without passing out, I went back to the subject of what the rest of them had missed.

"I can't believe none of you saw it," I voiced my disappointment.

Justin crouched so he was at my eye level as I sat on a chair in the corner of the kitchen.

"What, Felicity? What didn't we see?"

"Mr Moscovitch," I paused because I couldn't believe what I was about to say, "has a gun with him."

Justin's forehead creased in doubt. "A gun?"

He didn't believe me, but I knew what I had seen. "Yes, like a high-powered rifle or something," I struggled to describe it, my knowledge of guns almost nil, but with a snap of my fingers, I said, "A sniper rifle. That's what it was."

Chef O'Malley came to stand beside Justin, and Philippe was lurking a few feet away. They all heard what I said as did half a dozen or more of the chefs who stopped what they were doing to listen, until Chef O'Malley noticed their lack of activity.

"Get back to work!" she roared at them. "Those cheesecakes won't make themselves." Turning her attention back to me now that her staff was working faster than they had been before, she said, "What are we going to do about the lobster and steak, Felicity? I can manage without the lobster for a while, but the beef wellingtons must be made in advance. Danny is making the pastry for it now, and Sharon is on the mushroom duxelles ..." she let the sentence trail off, the urgency of her situation far more important than a gun I might have seen.

Forced to focus on a problem that needed to be solved, I acknowledged that while I felt an overwhelming desire to prove what I had seen and then find out what he was up to, the more important next action on my part was to rally my supply chain and get the food replaced.

Justin beat me to it.

"I'll make the calls," he announced with his phone in hand and the first number already dialled.

Thankful to have him with me, as he stepped away, I placed a hand on Chef O'Malley's elbow and guided her to one corner of the kitchen.

My mind was whirling; different and conflicting ideas sparking into life to whizz around and collide with each other. If I accepted that someone had taken Ernie, which I was far more prepared to do now that someone had decided to mess with the catering, then it led me to the conclusion that I was witnessing a deliberate attempt to derail the wedding.

That Mr Moscovitch was toting a firearm scared me senseless, yet it was my instant belief that he planned to use it on whoever was behind the misery his beloved daughter was now being forced to endure. I did not for one moment believe that he was behind the missing dog or the ruined food, but it wouldn't shock me to discover that the family was being targeted by one of his criminal rivals, perhaps in retribution for wrongs that he himself had committed against them.

Admittedly, I was guessing all of this, but his behaviour suggested I might be thinking along the right track.

Now out of earshot of everyone else, I quizzed Chef O'Malley.

"Have you seen anyone hanging around who shouldn't be here? I want you to gather all your staff together and ask them about it too." Chef was giving me a strange look that insisted I provide some further explanation. "I'm worried somebody might be trying to mess with this wedding."

The first name that came into my head was Primrose Green, another wedding planner and arguably the only other person I considered likely to get the contract for the royal wedding. There was more than enough market for both of us to play in, yet she had always attempted to undermine my business because she saw me as a threat. It would never occur to me to target one of her events. I felt certain I could not say the same of her.

"What exactly does that mean, Felicity?" asked Chef with a deep frown pinching her eyebrows together.

"Okay, you don't know this yet and there's no reason for me to have bothered you it with at any point today, but the bride's little dog has gone missing and she's refusing to get married without it."

"Gone missing? Like wandered off?"

I puffed out my cheeks as I searched for what I felt was an accurate or truthful answer.

"I was hoping so, but now I think maybe someone deliberately took him. She has an award-winning champion Pomeranian, and it was supposed to be the ring bearer today." I explained Ernie's importance with a sigh because though I had been attempting to resist it, I could already see that I was going to have to start investigating.

Unless by some stroke of luck Mindy and Buster were able to locate the tiny dog, I was going to have to put on my sleuthing hat and I already knew where I was going to start.

Proof of Life

Surreptitiously observing the hotel lobby and entrance from one corner of the library, Albert was surprised to see the two police officers leaving. They did not have Rex with them and the fact that they were leaving suggested that they were never here for him in the first place.

He sat and pondered that for a good few minutes before deciding there was no good reason to remain where he was. If the police were leaving the premises, then so could he. Albert had no idea what might have brought so many officers to the hotel, however it must have proven to be a false alarm because they had all left just as swiftly as they had arrived.

Gladly accepting that he had at least one more day of freedom, Albert felt himself relax. He had not been aware how stressed he felt until the tension began to flow away. Taking out his phone, he called his eldest son.

"Dad, where are you?" Gary wasted no time in firing off a question.

"If I don't tell you, son, you cannot be tempted to lie about it to anyone." Albert believed his children would protect him, but also that they could benefit most by convincing him to come in for questioning so his name could be cleared.

He wasn't going to do that. In his eyes it ran too great a risk that the people he was trying to save would suffer instead. He didn't know how many people were involved, but the small amount of research he conducted suggested it might be a dozen or more all held captive by whoever was behind the bizarre string of Gastrothief crimes.

"I just called to let you know that I am well and will be moving on shortly. I think it's best if I don't tell you where I'm going. Suffice it to say that I am heading to intercept agents of the Gastrothief. I know where they will be and when. If I am able to do so ... if I believe it will lead to the capture and arrest of their boss, I will make the appropriate calls and bring the authorities crashing down on them."

Sitting in his office in London, Gary scratched at his scalp and thought about what it might be that he could say to prevent his father from pursuing his potentially dangerous investigation. One of his father's friends, a retired RAF Wing Commander, had been shot by the same agents his father was now proposing to pursue. They were dangerous people, of that there could be no doubt.

Albert, feeling his son's silence, and knowing that Gary was about to try to talk some sense into him, led him down a different path.

"It's good to hear your voice, kiddo. Why don't you tell me about whatever case you're currently working on?" It was a regular question, an opener if you like that Albert would often fire at his three kids so they got to talk about their work. Each of them would regale him with stories that they would naturally embellish because they liked to see the sparkle of excitement in their father's eyes.

Accepting defeat, albeit temporarily, Gary hoped, he said, "Actually I've got quite the tale to tell. Have you ever heard of an author called Simon Slater?"

"Is he a horror novelist?" Albert dredged his memory, but wasn't sure he had his facts right. "Didn't he die in some grisly, mysterious manner?"

"That's exactly right, Dad. It was one of the strangest cases I've ever had. Let me tell you what happened ..."

Albert pushed back his chair and wandered from the library with his phone pressed against his ear. Listening with rapt fascination, he was still on the phone when he got to his room. Acting as casually as he could, he swiped his card against the door and turned the handle.

That Rex was missing became apparent before the door was even halfway open. The room had been cleaned, the bed neatly made, and his dog was nowhere to be seen.

"Everything all right, Dad?" Gary stopped what he was saying to react to the string of curse words his father had just uttered.

Albert crossed the room with fast strides, snatching Rex's lead from the side table before hurrying back out.

"Not entirely," he replied. "Sorry, son, I've got to go. I'll call you back later." Albert ended the call, thumbing the red button to cut Gary off mid-sentence. He would call him back when he got the chance, but right now he needed to find Rex.

The police didn't have him, and Albert felt quite certain that had anyone else attempted to take his dog against his will, the entire hotel would have known about it. A flash of panic made his heart beat super-fast for a couple of seconds before he forced himself to calm.

The spike of worry came from remembering that the Gastrothief's agents had tracked him to his house. That they had intended to kidnap, harm or possibly even kill him was one of the reasons Albert was now in hiding. For a brief moment he had questioned whether they might have somehow known he was here, and the only way that could happen was if they forced the information from the only person in the world who knew where he was.

Albert flipped through the contacts list in his phone and with an urgent finger stabbed the button to connect him with Wing Commander Roy Hope.

"Albert, old boy!" trumpeted Albert's old friend and neighbour as a greeting. "How's life on the run?"

That Roy had answered the phone and was clearly not speaking under duress had already provided the answer Albert sought.

Breathing a sigh of relief, Albert said, "I'm just checking in." There was no need to tell Roy about the police being here or that Rex had inexplicably escaped from his room. Now back out in the corridor and wondering which direction to head, Albert spotted the cleaner's cart parked outside a door two along from his. "Just wanted there to be someone in the world that knows that I'm okay. Rex and I will be moving on shortly, but I'll keep you posted on my progress."

"Be sure that you do, old boy. If you need any help with anything at all …"

"I'll call you if I do," Albert promised, ending the call quickly because the cleaner had just returned to her cart. "Hello," he called to get her attention. When she looked his way, Albert asked, "I don't suppose you've seen a large German Shepherd dog this morning, have you?"

SIDEKICKS

At that precise moment, Rex was in the hotel gardens, his nose to the ground as he followed the scent of a cat. It was the bulldog's scent he was attempting to acquire, but there were so many canine odours filling the space and conflicting to be dominant that each time he found it, he swiftly lost it again.

Backtracking to the point where he first crossed Buster's trail, Rex's nose detected a smell that at first confused him. He was smelling a cat, there could be no confusion about that. It was a mature female and clearly domesticated from the scent of humanity mingled in with the cat's natural aroma. However, hidden in the background, completely intertwined with the cat and human smells, was the odour of the bulldog.

Rex gave himself a moment to figure out how that could be, deciding after a while that the cat and dog must live together because the human smell mingled with the cat's odour also appeared with the bulldog's scent.

The cat smell was fresh, so Rex followed it. The trail grew stronger and easier to follow with each passing yard, until Rex came across a path and stopped to look around.

Using his eyes for once, he observed the dogs he could see in every direction. There had to be four dozen of them at least. There were humans about as well, gathered in small clumps to converse. Rex was about to set off again, intending to continue tracking the cat's scent trail, when he spotted a human he recognised.

It was the young female who had been out with the bulldog when Rex met him early this morning. Setting off towards her, Rex could only see her top half until she stepped out from behind a neatly trimmed hedgerow being led by the bulldog.

Pushing off with his back legs, Rex bounded over to them, a single bark all that was required to get Buster's attention.

"Has the missing dog been found yet?" Rex asked, his tail wagging in anticipation. Secretly, and though he knew it was a little wrong, he hoped the Pomeranian was still missing. It was a nice day; the sun shining down from a blue sky, and Rex wanted to be outside doing something, not stuck in his human's hotel room.

Pleased to see the German Shepherd, Buster said, *"No, there's no sign of him yet. Are you here to help?"* he asked. *"Two noses are better than one and all that."*

Rex said, "*Sure. I don't have anything else to do. Did I mention I used to be a police dog?*"

Buster flexed his eyebrows, a question forming instantly. "*Used to be? You're a little young to have retired, aren't you?*" Buster was wondering if the large German Shepherd had perhaps been injured in the line of duty and was forced to retire, but he didn't want to say that in case it sounded like he was suggesting it looked like Rex had something wrong with him.

Dismissively, Rex said, "*It's unimportant.*" He could have said that he was fired from the police dog service after the handlers refused to work with him. It would have been an honest answer, but Rex had learned that it just generated more questions. He had run rings around his human handlers, generally making them look stupid as he solved the crimes, cornered the criminals, and waited for them to perform the arrest.

Whatever he was going to say next was interrupted by the arrival of the cat he'd been trailing.

Mindy performed a double take upon seeing her aunt's cat saunter out of the bushes.

"Amber what are you doing here?" she asked even though she knew she wasn't going to get an answer. "How did you get out of the room even?"

Amber sashayed across the grass toward Buster, making a point of ignoring the giant German Shepherd dog he was talking to.

"*Solved the case yet have you, Buster?*" she asked in a teasing voice, knowing full well that he hadn't because she'd just heard him say so. "*Of course not,*" she answered for herself, getting in quickly to cut Buster off just as he was about to speak. "*This is going to require brains. Something you are sadly lacking in.*"

Taking a deep breath so he would not rise to the cat's goading, Buster asked, "*Why do you care if the little dog gets found? Since when did you care about anything much at all?*"

Amber chuckled at his question. "*Oh, I don't care about the dog, Buster. But if I let you solve this case, you'll just annoy me with it, so I think I'll demonstrate my superiority in an unequivocal manner by finding the missing dog first.*"

Buster could feel his top lip curling. "*You go ahead, Amber, and we shall see who finds Ernie first.*"

Amber turned around and began walking back towards the hotel, making sure to trail her tail beneath the German Shepherd's nose as a demonstration of how little the giant dog intimidated her.

"*Indeed, we shall,*" she called over her shoulder, taunting Buster with her final words.

"*Friend of yours?*" asked Rex.

Buster looked around for something he could bite or stomp on or perhaps just lift his leg against. Amber made his blood boil on a daily if not hourly basis.

"*That is the cat I am forced to live with,*" he replied through gritted teeth. Pushing Amber's taunts from his mind, he tried his best to think tranquil thoughts. It lasted for a few seconds before the need to kill something returned. His mood wasn't helped by the attitude he got from Cerberus earlier.

The Doberman had talked down to him as if he were a peasant in the company of the king.

Dropping his voice an octave, and forcing it to rasp, he growled, "*It's Devil Dog time.*"

Rex twitched a single eyebrow, "*Huh?*"

Speaking mostly to himself, Buster growled, "*It's Devil Dog time. That means I'm giving my superhero persona free rein to tackle this investigation as he sees fit.*" Buster was mentally preparing himself to do all that was needed to ensure he emerged victorious. Picturing the cheers and adulations from both the show dogs here today and their humans, he could see himself leading Ernie the Pomeranian back to his human. A new thought occurred to him. "*If you're going to be my sidekick, you'll have to have a superhero name too.*"

"*I think I'll just stick with Rex, if it's all the same to you,*" said Rex. Trying to get away from the bulldog's strange ideas. Wondering if perhaps he ought to just go at it alone, Rex started walking again, this time heading towards a gaggle of dogs he could see near a large oak tree.

"*Squad Dog,*" Buster tried out a new name for Rex. He needed something cool, and that paired elegantly with Devil Dog. He'd occasionally teamed up with the dog next door, a Chihuahua who called himself Hell Pup. Squad Dog was a terrible name, Buster decided, testing out, "*Sir Killalot*," to see how that sounded before dismissing it too.

His paws operating on autopilot, Buster followed Rex, dragging Mindy along behind him.

"Where are we going now, Buster?" she wanted to know. Walking the dog outside in the sunshine was more fun than dealing with the long list of jobs her Aunt Felicity would have for her if she went back inside, but she also knew she couldn't drag this out for too much longer.

Maybe the work was getting done without her there, and maybe it wasn't. She liked her job. She liked working with her aunt, who was way cooler than her mum. At the thought of her mum, Mindy uttered an expletive. She'd completely forgotten that she was here too.

SISTErLY LOVE

"Where are we going again, Mrs Philips?" Philippe wanted to know as I led him through the hotel.

Over my shoulder I said, "I already told you, Philippe. I'm worried someone is attempting to mess with this wedding so as the wedding planner it is *my* responsibility to figure out who it is."

"And that means breaking into Mr Moscovitch's room?"

I twisted my head around to glare at him. "Shhh! It is not just the wedding I am worried about, Philippe. If Mr Moscovitch is being targeted by one of his ..." I searched for a polite term, "rivals, and decides to take matters into his own hands ... well, let's just say I'd rather prevent that from happening."

"And you think he has a gun."

Fifteen minutes had passed since I saw him take the rifle from the other man in the car park. Was he a business associate? A local arms dealer whose phone number Mr Moscovitch just happened to have? I had watched the two men shake hands before the arms dealer or whatever he was got in his car and drove off. The father of the bride then took what appeared to be a heavy bag of golf clubs and carried it into the hotel. The bag was the kind that came with a hood to completely encapsulate the head of the clubs and made sure no one could see what was inside.

His daughter was getting married today, what on earth did he need a set of golf clubs for? It was far too suspicious.

Certain that someone was trying to prevent the wedding from happening, I was convinced there were only two possibilities. Either the events I was witness to were the result of Mr Moscovitch's criminal lifestyle, or it was the slightly more palatable but equally annoying dirty tactics of Primrose Green.

As the wedding planner I had duplicate cards for two rooms: the bridal suite and the room the bride's parents were staying in. Under normal circumstances, I would only enter the rooms if the persons staying there were inside or had expressly given me their permission to enter their room.

These were not normal circumstances.

Believing that Mr Moscovitch would not want me anywhere near his room if he had weapons in there, I planned to find out where he was and then position Philippe as a sentry while I inspected the bag of golf clubs to find and photograph the evidence I required.

I wasn't going to call the police though. Goodness no. I needed this wedding to pass without the press taking interest because there had been a triple homicide. Honestly, when I found the gun, I wasn't entirely sure what I was going to do, but hoped I might be able to speak quietly with Mrs Moscovitch about my concerns.

That was for later, right now I needed to find Mr Moscovitch.

My phone rang, the sound of it muffled by my handbag until I lifted it out to see who was calling. I expected it to be Justin to let me know that he'd secured fresh supplies, or perhaps Mindy telling me that the little dog had been found.

It was neither of those. It was my sister.

Following an argument with her husband, she'd stormed from the house, taking Mindy with her, only to realise she had nowhere to go, and all her credit cards were in her husband's name. Attempting to prove that she didn't need him, even though she'd never really earned her own money at any point in her life, she decided to move in with me.

Somehow, I had no say in the matter, and I guess I have no one to blame for that but myself. My elder sister has always bossed me around, and I have always let her. We hadn't spoken much in the last couple of decades, our relationship dwindling to the point where I would send her a Christmas card and not get one in return. I suppose it speaks volumes about my needs and desires that I found her choice to ignore me disappointing.

Thumbing the green button, I lifted my phone to my ear.

"Finally awake then are we, Ginny?" I sneered, feeling no need to exchange pleasantries.

"Someone got out of the wrong side of the bed this morning, didn't they?" Ginny shot back smartly. "I just called down to room service and they said they're no longer serving breakfast."

I waited, expecting there to be something else she might add to make a question out of her statement.

"Well?" she snapped, clearly expecting me to have reacted already.

Feeling my anger rising, and my jaw clenching, I managed to speak at a normal volume when I said, "That's what happens when you don't get up until nearly noon, Ginny. Perhaps you shouldn't have drunk so much last night. Thank you so much for putting it all on my tab."

"Oh, do stop complaining. You are rich, Felicity. You might not have anything else in your life, but you do have money."

I thought about trying to strangle the phone.

"I need some breakfast, Felicity. Surely you can use your influence here to sort that out for me. Don't you have an entire catering team in the kitchen at your beck and call?"

"That is not what they're here for, Ginny. They have a lot of work to do and are under enough pressure already. I'm not taking one of them away to make you a bacon sandwich." I was all but spitting out my words. Under pressure anyway from the imminent royal wedding announcement, with the additional pressure of a big wedding day bearing down on top of me, the unpredictable problems I was now facing because there was a wedding saboteur on the loose were driving me to act a little irrationally. I am not normally given to displaying my anger, though I suppose when it comes to my sister there is a hard-wired shortcut to it already in place.

"Goodness, you are a grumpy little lady this morning." My diminutive stature was another thing that as children she had regularly used against me. "However is it that you came to be a successful business woman, Felicity? You cannot even keep your emotions under control. I'll attend to my own needs then since my sister cannot be bothered to help me." With that she hung up the phone, and my blood quietly boiled inside my veins.

I could have left her at home while I was away for the weekend working with her daughter Mindy, but I felt it far too likely my arrogant, superior sister would begin to rearrange things in my house. She had been staying with me for a week while she attempted to negotiate life not living with her husband, but rather than be grateful for the roof I put above her head, within minutes of arriving, she was advising me on what I should do to change the décor, and how my bathroom needed to be improved.

With that in mind, and fearing that I might return to find interior decorators hanging new wallpaper in my living room at my expense if I left her behind, I insisted she come with us.

Surprisingly, she volunteered to help, saying that Mindy always talked about the work as if it were interesting - Ginny's tone suggested that anything I had a hand in would be anything but. However, the moment I attempted to assign her a task I felt within her capability, she vanished for two hours and was found halfway through a bottle of gin in the hotel bar.

I was still cursing my sister's name when I approached the bridal suite. I paused a few yards short to discuss my plan with Philippe.

"Checking on the bride several times throughout the hours leading up to the ceremony is completely normal of course," I was using this as a teaching moment for my new assistant. He was familiar with the wedding industry, but until recently had been viewing it through the eyes of a makeup artist who would be employed to ensure the bride and other members of the bridal party looked flawless. "By now she should be getting hair and makeup, and I usually use these moments to make sure the bride isn't drinking too much champagne."

I'd had far too many events when one bottle of champagne to celebrate the day had become four and brides who were smashed almost to the point that the ceremony needed to be called off. It tended to be the younger ones with older siblings and mature friends all of drinking age.

It rarely happened when the bridesmaids were children.

"Really what I'm doing is making sure that Mr Moscovitch is with his daughter."

"What if he isn't?" Philippe asked a pertinent question.

"Then I'll have to surreptitiously ask where he is." To stave off any further questions, I strode purposefully towards the door to the bridal suite. I could hear the argument raging on the other side before I had a chance to knock.

OLD ACQUAINTANCES

Albert stopped a staff member to ask why there were so many dogs at the hotel. Heading directly to his room when he checked in the previous evening, and with the exception of his breakfast only going out so he could exercise Rex, he had no idea there was a wedding set to take place at the hotel today.

The wedding itself was not a shock, the number of dogs involved was, however, a little surprising.

Standing outside the hotel and feeling a little exposed as well as slightly exasperated because he was supposed to be packing their things and leaving, Albert was scanning the grounds for his dog. It was nearing noon, and if he didn't get on his way shortly, there was no chance he would make Cornwall before nightfall.

"Where are you, Rex?" he asked the air. Swift visual calculation told Albert he was seeing at least forty dogs. Some of them were on their leads, three were in handbags. One was in a pushchair of all things and wearing sunglasses. The dog in the pushchair was hard to see, but Albert believed he was looking at a French Bulldog. The remainder were roaming free, sniffing here and there, gathering in groups, but none of them, Albert noted, were chasing toys. The complete absence of frisbees, tennis balls, or even the obligatory stick made the scene look somehow wrong.

Scanning from left to right, Albert saw dogs of all breeds, but there was no sign of Rex.

Unwilling to linger too long, Albert pushed on. He needed to find his dog and do so quickly. Heading directly for a gaggle of people, he called out just as he got to them.

"I say. Please excuse my interruption. I don't suppose anyone has seen a German Shepherd, have they? Male. Quite a large fellow."

"German Shepherd?" repeated a man wearing a tweed suit. In his thirties, to Albert's mind the suit made the man look like he was trying to be old before his time or had perhaps borrowed it from his grandfather.

Albert's eyes were drawn away when another person spoke.

"I saw one go by a couple of minutes ago," said a woman in a wax jacket. "He was with a young woman in sportswear and a bulldog?" she said it as a question, seeking to confirm that sounded right to the old man asking the questions.

Albert didn't know if that meant the dog she'd seen was Rex or not, but he remembered seeing a young woman who matched the description earlier. She was with the bulldog, he recalled, twirling a set of nunchucks while she waited for the dog to do his business.

"Thank you. Did you see which way they went?"

The woman in the wax jacket indicated a direction and Albert continued on his way, muttering to himself about how a person his age shouldn't have to spend so much time rushing around.

The hotel, a former stately home, long since abandoned by the family who built it more than two hundred years ago, was surrounded on all four sides by sculpted gardens. Wide open lawns were divided into separate areas by rows of pleached trees, carefully clipped bushes, and walls intended to give some areas a sense of intimacy. One garden, Albert noted as he passed it, was filled with the biggest marquee he had ever seen. The canvas was so brilliantly white it had to be brand new, and when the cogs aligned in his head, he saw that it was for the wedding he now knew was due to take place later today.

Albert couldn't know it, but the hotel's grounds and ornate gardens were one of the reasons Felicity pushed her local clients to book the spa/retreat as their wedding venue. The walled gardens could be booked in advance and in warmer months, the receptions were often held outside in the open air, a hog roast or a barbeque replacing the more traditional seated banquet.

Albert left one garden and arrived in another. There were a few more dogs here, but the bulk of them were behind him now.

There was still no sign of Rex, but Albert spotted a man standing by himself. Albert made to move in his direction, hoping to ask the same question about whether he'd spotted a German Shepherd in the recent past, but he found a frown forming on his brow because the man's gaze was already aimed undeniably his way. Squarely his way, and it looked like he had a question of his own.

Albert's cop brain, honed by decades in the job, placed the man in his mid-fifties. His hair was brown and beginning to recede. He kept it cut short on the top and even shorter at the back and sides in a style that reminded Albert of his own hair when he was a constable in uniform. Wearing grey trousers and a belt that had seen better days, his top half was covered by a shirt, jacket, tie, and coat. They looked too big for him, giving Albert the impression the man might have lost weight recently. At five feet and eight inches, he was a little on the short side, but hadn't stooped to wearing Cuban heels as Albert had seen other men do.

"Hello," Albert smiled as he came closer. "I'm looking for a German Shepherd. I don't suppose you've seen one. It might be in the company of a bulldog and a young lady in sports clothing."

The man didn't answer straight away. Instead, he seemed to need a minute to consider his answer. His lips were pursed, and he was staring hard, directly into Albert's eyes.

Albert had expected an answer. It would be a 'yes' or a 'no', but the scruffy-looking man wasn't saying anything, and it was becoming not only rude, but also annoying.

About to question if there was something wrong, which would lead to a rebuke Albert could already feel forming, he was cut off when the man made a small, thoughtful noise with his mouth and began to speak.

"Ironically, I was looking for a German Shepherd myself," the man remarked.

It was the last thing Albert expected him to say.

"Or rather," the scruffy man continued, "I'm looking for an older gentleman travelling with a German Shepherd."

Albert's heart snapped out a staccato beat, the clues delivering the simple truth of his situation – he was talking to a police detective. Inside, he sighed, accepting his fate, and on the surface, he nodded his head, wordlessly congratulating the man on some excellent work.

"What gave me away?" he asked, curious to hear how the man had so easily tracked him to the venue.

Albert wasn't expecting a set of handcuffs to appear, but the right thing for the detective to do at this juncture was read Albert his rights, so it came as something of a shock when the man did neither.

"I think perhaps we should have a chat," he suggested, though Albert knew it was nothing of the sort. "I'm Detective Sergeant Mike Atwell," he put out his hand for Albert to shake.

Albert felt his forehead crease. "Mike Atwell?"

DS Atwell added, "I doubt very much that you remember me. I was a young constable in uniform when you retired. I believe you only spoke to me once and that was to tear a strip off me."

Albert felt his cheeks colouring. There was no good reason to feel embarrassed; he was certain he'd never had harsh words for any of the officers he worked with unless they genuinely deserved it. Nevertheless, it was a lifetime ago, and though the name sounded familiar, he could not recall a younger version of the man he was talking to nor remember the incident to which he was alluding.

DS Atwell waved a dismissive hand to stop Albert feeling the need to comment.

"Don't worry," he said, "I deserved it at the time. I'm nearing retirement myself, actually." An uneasy silence fell as both men looked at each other, each waiting for the other to make a move. After a few seconds Mike said, "So, tea while we chat?"

The surprise Albert felt manifested only as a slight rising of his eyebrows. He knew for certain that what DS Atwell should be doing was performing an arrest. However, that clearly wasn't his immediate intent. With no idea why that was the case and no option about what he did now anyway, Albert followed where the police officer led.

Hair and Makeup

"Mrs Philips this is not a good time," commented the mother of the bride the moment she clocked who was coming through the door. On a day when she ought to be looking jubilant and glowing and possibly even slightly tipsy from a glass of pre-lunch champagne, Mrs Moscovitch instead looked a little bit beaten. Of Mr Moscovitch there was no sign. It was not what I hoped for, and it was quite clear that I could not immediately question where he was. There were other issues to deal with first.

I felt no option but to argue. "My apologies, Mrs Moscovitch, it was impossible to approach the bridal suite without overhearing the conversation coming from within."

Just as I predicted, the beauty team had arrived to get started on the hair and makeup. With less than three hours remaining before the bride was due to walk down the aisle, there really was no time for delay and it was quite clear that the bride was nowhere near ready.

Donna was still sitting on the chaise longue, her feet tucked up underneath her to be buried by the bathrobe she still wore. Her eyes were puffy from crying and her nose was bulbous and red from constantly being blown.

This wouldn't do at all.

Around the room, Donna's three bridesmaids and her sister - the maid of honour - were all in various stages of preparation. None of them had their dresses on yet - it was far too early for that, but their hair had been neatly braided with flowers so the three girls matched even though their hair shade and lengths were different. Denise would be wearing a variation of the same dress as the three bridesmaids and her hair was to be braided in a different manner.

Much toing and froing had gone back and forth over these small details in the months preceding today, and though it ate up more of my time than I considered it to be worth, it was nevertheless what I got paid for.

What I really needed in the bridal suite was my number one assistant, Mindy. On such a day as we were having, I would deploy her to make sure the bridal party's preparations continued at an appropriate pace while I attended to other tasks.

I whispered to Philippe that he should stay put next to the door and crossed the room to speak directly with Donna - she was the focus of the day.

"Donna, dear, we only have a few hours to get you ready."

"Ready for what?" she sobbed. "I'm not getting married without Ernie."

"I understand, dear. But we have a lot of people looking for him and I'm sure he will be found. If we do not get on with the task of getting you ready, we run the risk of ruining the ceremony." Okay, so I was laying it on a little thick by suggesting the entire day might be ruined. However, Donna needed a little shock in my opinion. "The makeup artists and hairdressers have other appointments to go to." That wasn't true; I'd booked them for the entire day and shot a warning glance to stay quiet when a few of them looked my way. "If we don't at least prepare you to walk down the aisle, when Ernie is returned to you, as I am sure he will be, well let's just say you should have a look in the mirror and decide if this is how you wish to be photographed on your big day."

Mrs Moscovitch came to stand behind her daughter, placing a hand on her shoulder where she sat.

"Mrs Philips is right, dear. Ernie is bound to show up. The little scamp probably just went chasing lady doggies."

Sensing that they needed to join in, Donna's three best friends all came to crowd her at the chaise longue.

"Your mum is right, Donna," said Ellie. "Ernie is bound to show up shortly and all this worry will have been for nothing"

Juniper joined in. "You get to marry Damien today in that amazing dress. Everyone is here."

"It's going to be wonderful," added Christy. "But we have to get you ready."

"But where is he?" Donna wailed, meaning her dog.

Denise, the one person in the room who was yet to say anything, raised a hand to stop her makeup artist from working.

"Yes, where is Ernie?" she questioned as she rose to her feet. "Move out of the way," she barked at Ellie, so she could come to sit on the carpet next to Donna. Taking her younger sister's hand, she looked at the other women scornfully. "I don't think any of you understand quite what that little dog means to Donna."

Taken aback, Mrs Moscovitch had a stern face when she replied, "Of course we do, Denise."

"Then why are you pushing her so hard, mother? It's clear Donna is distraught. It's just a wedding. It doesn't matter if it gets postponed. Are you proposing to have Donna walk up the aisle with her tears tracking mascara down over her cheeks? What if Ernie isn't found in time for the ceremony?"

In response to the question, Donna let out a huge sob and descended into tears again disproving my theory that they ought by now to be all cried out.

Denise pulled her into a hug.

I puffed out my cheeks and bit down on my frustration. This was not how I wanted today to go. I needed to get Donna cleaned up, made up, and into her dress. It was, however, quite apparent, that this wasn't going to happen until I found the missing Pomeranian.

The conclusion led me neatly back to my belief that this had to have something to do with Mr Moscovitch's shady business activities. I was going to have to figure out what he was up to.

We had reached a stalemate regarding the bride's preparation, and that was a problem, but it also gave me an opportunity.

"Where is Mr Moscovitch?"

Breedism

On the other side of the hotel and outside in the gardens, Mindy was letting Buster lead her where he wanted to go while she was attempting to have a phone conversation with her mother.

"I can't come right now, Mum, I'm working. I thought you were going to be helping me out today. Wasn't that the plan?"

Mindy knew that her mum was in the wrong regarding her parents' marriage. Dad had always been the breadwinner and very generous in his willingness to let mum do more or less whatever she wanted with her time and the money that he put into the joint account. Even as a little girl she'd had to endure her mother's tantrums, listening to her parents arguing downstairs while she hid in her bedroom.

Mum wanted more money and refused to see why her husband felt it necessary to save. She wanted a better car even though she was already driving a brand new whatever it might happen to be at the time.

And she never lifted a finger, which was what created most of the arguments.

Dad would come home late after a long day in court to find he needed to start doing housework. The sink would be full of dishes, there would be nothing to eat, and were he ever foolish enough to highlight these shortcomings to his wife he would then suffer the cold shoulder for days to come.

That it had taken him this long to snap was why he had snapped so hard. Nevertheless, Mindy only had one mum and despite her failings, she loved her very dearly.

Mindy had called to check on what her mother was up to and to make sure that she was out of bed. Choosing to drown her sorrows last night, it had taken Mindy some effort to convince her mother to retire when she was only mostly drunk. Had she imbibed much more, she would be suffering severely this morning.

Now, as was her habit, Mindy's mother was acting as if nothing had happened.

"I'm not really feeling in the mood for it today, Mindy, and your aunt doesn't really deserve my help."

Mindy just rolled her eyes at that remark because her mother was right. Aunt Felicity really didn't deserve to have to put up with her sister's 'help'.

"Okay, Mum. I've got quite a bit to be getting on with today. I'll catch up with you in a little while, yes?"

Mindy heard her mother's exaggerated sigh. "I suppose so, Mindy. Everyone is too busy for me it seems. My sister couldn't even see her way to help me get some food. Weddings," she muttered, "such ridiculous nonsense. Please let me know if you can squeeze your mother into your busy diary later today."

Mindy frowned at her phone. Her mother had chosen to end the call in the rudest of manners. At nineteen, she recognised that she didn't have enough life or relationship experience to fully comprehend how her mother might feel at this time. Yet she had attempted to suggest that her parents' marriage wasn't beyond saving if her mother was prepared to make a few changes to her lifestyle. She wanted nothing more than for things to go back to how they were. Was she being selfish? She didn't think so. In fact, she felt like she was the sole voice of reason.

Muttering to herself as she put her phone back in the stretchy pocket on her right hip, Mindy turned her attention back to the dogs and was surprised to find they had multiplied in number when she was not looking.

Rex had led the way to a group of dogs with the intention of quizzing them on what they might have smelled or seen. There were at least a dozen of them all huddled in a group. Perhaps he could recruit some of them to assist him in the search for the missing Pomeranian.

However, when he suggested the concept, a muscular Doberman laughed in his face.

"You want to recruit us?" the Doberman chuckled, the idea clearly ridiculous to him.

Buster sidled up next to Rex. "This is Cerberus," he murmured so only Rex would hear. "He's a bit of a dick."

"I'd rather think it ought to be the other way around, don't you?" Cerberus remarked in a knowing tone. He was playing up for the dogs around him, that much was clear, and they were looking at him as if he were their leader.

Rex wasn't about to be spoken down to. "You have experience in these matters, do you?" he asked. "Led many investigations? I'm a former police dog. This is precisely what I do. I only ask that you assist me because what we should all be focused on is the successful recovery of the missing dog."

Cerberus made a shocked face and then burst out laughing.

When he could speak again, he said, "Wow! How deliciously working class. He used to be a police dog, everyone."

Rex waited patiently as the dogs surrounding Cerberus sniggered dutifully.

Buster curled his lip and lunged. He'd had quite enough of Cerberus's superior attitude and classism. Aiming for a front paw, his teeth snapped together in empty space when Mindy yanked his lead backwards.

The failed attempt only made Cerberus howl with laughter.

"Oh, goodness. You two should be a comedy double act," he played to his audience a little more.

Now bored with the Doberman, Rex took a pace towards him. He wasn't on the lead and had no idea where his human was. Not only that, he knew that he weighed a good few pounds more than the lean, muscular, black and tan dog and was quite prepared to prove a point if it became necessary.

"I think you're being a little rude," he growled. "Your focus should be on the missing dog."

Still acting as though he found Rex amusing, Cerberus said, "Oh, but it is. We were just discussing how glad we are that the ridiculous little toy dog is gone and how fervently we hope he never resurfaces." Cerberus dropped his amused tone and offered Rex a serious expression. "You're a pastoral dog though; you get it. Dogs like us have purpose. We have dignity. We could defend our humans if the need arose. Toy dogs, well, they're just so … pointless."

Rex felt his upper lip curling. He'd met other dogs with breedism issues, and he hated how it made him feel ugly inside to witness.

There were a lot of dogs on Cerberus's side of the equation, but Rex had decided he was going to teach the handsome Doberman a swift lesson in humility anyway. A quick nip on the ear should do it. Draw a little blood, make the dog yelp, and that should swiftly alter how the other dogs perceived him. They would instantly question if he was really their alpha.

Rex's muscles bunched, his back legs getting ready to launch him forward when he felt a hand suddenly loop itself through his collar.

"I think perhaps we'll just go somewhere else," said Mindy who had been watching the exchange with curiosity. She didn't know who the German Shepherd belonged to, yet he seemed to have chosen to tag along with Buster.

There would be an owner around here somewhere and it was almost certainly one of the wedding guests. It wouldn't do to be associated with a running dog battle in the middle of the hotel gardens.

Pulling Rex away by his collar she encouraged him, "Come along. Let's leave these dogs here." she checked to make sure they were not following.

Hooting and jeering as Rex and Buster were led away, Cerberus called out, "Ta ta now. Run along, little doggies. Such good boys."

Vibrating from the rage he felt, Buster growled, "If I get the chance, I'm going to scent mark his head."

Rex also had thoughts regarding how he might repay Cerberus, but it involved a large rubber dog toy and a run up and cannot be described on these pages lest they spontaneously combust.

Behind them as they were led away, Cerberus and his pack of dogs continued in their merriment. All except one dog who, possessing a mind of her own, chose to detach herself from the group and follow the bulldog and the German Shepherd.

SHARKS AND ASSASSINS

"Mrs Philips are you sure this is a good idea?"

I paused, my right hand gripping the handle to Mr Moscovitch's room and turned my head to reply to Philippe's question.

"A good idea? Of course it's not a good idea! You heard the bride though. She's not getting married until we find her dog. I have no idea what might have happened to him, and since I've had no update from Mindy, I think it's safe to assume that Buster has had no luck in locating him. I don't know that Mr Moscovitch is in any way involved, but I know for certain that he's up to something. I intend to find out what that is in the hope that it leads me to figure out who might be behind Ernie's disappearance."

Sucking in a sharp breath as I committed to what I was planning to do, I swiped the key card against the door lock and went inside. I caught a final glance at Philippe through the closing door, his wide eyes and a worried expression echoing what I felt.

That no one seemed to know where Mr Moscovitch was at this time felt like further evidence that he was up to no good.

"Golf clubs," I said to myself, rotating slowly on the spot as I scanned around the room. There was no sign of the red and white leather bag I'd seen him take from his car – the one with the rifle in it. Biting my lip, I set about searching the room.

Philippe was standing guard outside and would knock on the door to let me know if someone was coming. I wasn't overly worried about getting caught because I had a readily concocted excuse. If Mr or Mrs Moscovitch came, I was going to tell them that we were setting him and his wife up to find a gift in the morning and I was looking for the best place to hide it. I would explain - lying through my teeth - that this was a standard practise for my firm and something we did for every mother and father of the bride.

Of course, if I were to be discovered and forced to employ the lie, I would then need to spend some money on something spectacular, but that would be nothing more than a minor inconvenience.

In little more than a minute, I was able to confirm that the golf bag was not in the room. There simply weren't enough hiding places where it could be stashed. It wasn't as if it would fit in a drawer.

Pulling a face as I scratched my head and trying to figure out where else I should look, I jolted when I looked out the window and spotted Mr

Moscovitch in the grounds of the hotel. He was in the company of a man who looked like a mortician. A solemn face, a pale complexion, and a string bean body combined to give me the impression he was an underworld assassin. Heck, maybe people in the trade nicknamed him 'the undertaker'.

The sight of Donna's father handing over a wad of notes stole my breath away. He was paying cash for something, a sure-fire way to make sure the transaction could never be traced or proven. First, I watched him buy a gun, now I was watching him hire a killer.

Okay, I knew I was jumping to conclusions. Maybe just a little, but that didn't mean I wasn't one hundred percent right.

The cadaverous looking man in the sunglasses dipped his head in salute, slipped the wad of cash inside his jacket and walked away without a word.

What the heck was I seeing? If Mr Moscovitch was hiring an assassin, who was the target?

The sound of the door opening tore me from my thoughts in much the same way that a trumpet in the ear will take a sleeping person from their state of slumber to fully awake and utterly terrified.

I spun around, my heart in my mouth as I fought against my panic so I could deliver my lie without looking like a thief caught in a spotlight.

Questioning what might have happened to Philippe, I tried to force my face to smile. Convinced I must look like I was suffering gastric distress, imagine my horror when a head popped around the edge of the door and I found myself staring at Vince.

A muscle by my left eye twitched; a tic Vince's shark-infested smile always seemed to inspire, kicking in before he even spoke.

I could feel my eyes narrowing without me asking them to. I liked Vince ... sometimes. Sort of. Actually, I found myself constantly vacillating from thinking I might consider entertaining a fledgling relationship with him, though the idea still terrified me, and looking around for a bucket of water I could pour over his head.

I had warmed to him, that much was true. Partly that was because he saved my life and then claimed to be in love with me. He'd been concussed at the time, but I also believed it was the first time he'd ever been truly honest with me.

His grin entered the room, followed a few seconds later by the man himself. As the door swung wide, I saw Philippe's sheepish and apologetic expression. I didn't assign any blame to him for failing to warn me; Vince was far from easy to manage.

"What are you doing here, Mr Slater?" I demanded to know, opting to not mince my words or sugar coat them.

My attitude did nothing to dent his smile. "Mr Slater? That's a little formal isn't it, darling? I rather hope you keep it up though for when we advance to the bedroom stage of our relationship."

I must have insisted he stop employing pet names for me a hundred times and had given up doing so because it just encouraged him. Instead, I just narrowed my eyes a little more.

"I am here to rescue you, Felicity," he continued when I said nothing. "I heard the call to respond to a missing child. Can I assume that since the police are not here that the situation has been resolved?"

Philippe's face crinkled with confusion, but I knew what Vince was talking about. He was a private investigator and security specialist. A bunch of people worked for him, and he had someone permanently tuned to the police band. That he knew where I was working this weekend and had someone alert him when they heard the police rolling in my direction came as no surprise.

"There never was a missing child," I updated him. "The bride's dog is missing."

Vince's smile widened; he was waiting for me to deliver a punchline.

"You're serious!" he choked on a laugh a few seconds later. "Wow, what did Chief Inspector Quinn make of that?"

I wanted to ask how Vince knew Quinn was heading the team that came here, but to do so would just give him ammunition to say something mysterious and annoying. Instead, I just answered his question.

"He tried to blame me."

Vince flipped his eyebrows, demonstrating how unsurprising my statement was. Changing subjects, he said, "What are you doing in here anyway, Felicity? Looking for the dog?"

"Not exactly. I think the father is involved in organised crime and that the dog might have been taken by one of his rivals." I saw the doubtful look in Vince's eyes. "I saw him take a gun from someone. They had their cars parked next to each other with the boot lids up to hide what they were doing. It looked like a rifle, and he put it into a bag of golf clubs so he could bring it into the hotel without anyone questioning it."

Vince was trying hard not to frown, but said, "How sure are you that it wasn't just a bag of golf clubs?"

"I saw a gun!" I insisted.

Vince raised his hands in surrender and was about to say something until I kept going because there was more to tell.

"Aaaaaand," I crossed the room to look out the window again, "he's just been outside handing cash to someone who looked like a hired assassin."

Now Vince's face registered surprise. It quickly turned quizzical, his eyebrows knitting together before he asked, "What exactly does a hired assassin look like?"

Okay, so he had me there. I wanted to say that one would look just like the tall, thin, cadaverous man I'd seen through the window, but obviously, the answer was someone who killed people for a living would do anything but stand out. They would look like no one; the kind of person you walked by without noticing.

"He was being handed a wad of cash!" I repeated. "It had to be five hundred pounds. At least," I added, suddenly thinking it didn't sound like a lot of money.

Vince was already picking holes in my ideas. "I believe the average contract killer earns a tad more than that per murder."

I grimaced at him, showing Vince my teeth because I couldn't think of anything to say, and Vince had to hide his face as he sniggered at me. Before I could find something to throw at him, he started moving.

"Okay, let's toss the room. If there is something here to find ..." He pointed a finger at Philippe. "Watch the corridor, kid. Call out if anyone is coming."

Philippe's eyes bugged from his head as he stood in the doorway and watched the besuited, middle-aged private investigator methodically work his way around the room.

In just a couple of minutes, Vince had swept through Mr and Mrs Moscovitch's belongings and was content there was nothing of interest squirrelled away beneath their socks or anywhere else.

"Hmmm," Vince looked around thoughtfully. "You said he looks like a criminal. What does he look like?"

On the spot, I thought about how to describe Mr Moscovitch. Struggling for words, my thoughts were interrupted when Vince held out his phone. There was a picture of my client on it. He was wearing a dark suit and sunglasses and looked as dangerous as ever. He'd been caught in a photographer's flashbulb as he left a club somewhere late at night – typical gangster activity to my mind.

Seeing the recognition on my face, Vince asked, "You really don't know who that is?"

I looked up at him. "No, should I?"

Philippe volunteered, "I do."

Vince waved him into silence and crossed the room to whisper something in my young assistant's ear.

Turning back to me when he got a nod from Philippe, Vince's face was serious.

"Gregor Moscovitch is a seriously dangerous man, Felicity. I don't know how you scored his daughter's wedding, but you need to consider vetting your clients in the future."

I found myself swallowing hard as terrible unease gripped me. I'd suspected since I first met him, but had never once thought to confirm my beliefs.

"Listen," Vince made me look at him. "Whatever you do, you cannot let on that you know. Gregor Moscovitch has gone to a lot of effort to ensure the police cannot touch him. He's the kind of person who makes witnesses vanish before they can testify against him. Obviously, it's too late for you to walk away now, so you need to keep quiet, get through this, and hope he doesn't call you next time he wants a wedding organised."

My heart was beating like a drum.

Vince angled his feet toward the door. "We should probably leave. Am I right to guess you would like some help to find the missing doggy?"

wanted, but innocent

In a quiet corner of the hotel, at a table set with two chairs, Detective Sergeant Mike Atwell was pouring tea into two white, porcelain teacups.

"Sugar?" he asked, placing the teapot back onto the silver tray and picking up the tongs with a sugar cube wedged between them.

Albert shook his head. "No, thank you." He loathed sweet tea.

Mike dropped the first cube into his own cup and chased it with a second. Swapping the tongs for the teaspoon on his saucer, he proceeded to stir, and while his right arm made swirling motions in the dark liquid, he fixed his gaze upon the elderly man sitting opposite.

"Why don't you tell me why Chief Inspector Quinn has a bee in his bonnet when it comes to you, Mr Smith. There is a warrant out for your arrest, a suggestion that you have ties to a terrorist incident that took place in Whitstable last night, and I keep hearing the word 'Gastrothief'."

Albert picked up his teacup and took a sip. The liquid was still too hot to drink so he put it down again.

Given the opportunity to explain, Albert chose to go all the way back to the start.

"My wife died last year."

"I'm sorry to hear that," Mike responded automatically.

Albert acknowledged the words with a small head motion and pressed on, "We had been married a long time and I felt a little lost in the house without her. I also discovered that I had no idea how to cook," he added with a rueful smile. "Petunia was always the one in the kitchen and she ... she produced the most amazing meals every single day." More than a year later, Albert still found it hard to talk about. He took a moment to gather himself. "A year to the day of her passing, I packed a small suitcase and a backpack, and I walked out of my front door. I was going on a trip, a culinary tour, if you will.

Over the course of the next thirty minutes, Albert told the detective sergeant all about his plan to visit the hometowns and birthplaces of his favourite foods and how he set out to learn how to make them all for himself. It hadn't gone entirely to plan.

In fact, the plan went sideways on the first day when he arrived in Melton Mowbray to discover a murder had taken place at the very establishment in which he was attending a pork pie making class.

The Gastrothief thing came later, Albert slowly becoming aware that there had to be someone operating in the background.

Mike Atwell listened with great interest, interrupting only twice to clarify points before encouraging Albert to carry on. The tale was fanciful and ridiculous. It was so bizarre and unbelievable that it had to be true.

When Albert finished speaking, he had brought Mike up to the present day, explaining about his gunfight with Tanya and Baldwin just a few hours ago, and how he was on the run from them just as much as he was hiding from the police.

"Regardless of what anyone, especially Chief Inspector Quinn, has to say on the matter, the Gastrothief is completely real. I probably should have come up with a better name for him, but whoever he is, and whatever reason he might have for stealing food and equipment, and kidnapping chefs and food experts, there can be no denying he exists now. Not after last night."

"Because of Tanya and Baldwin," Mike confirmed what Albert was saying. "You don't know who they are though?"

Albert huffed out a hard breath of frustration. "Nope."

"And there are no pictures of them."

"Nope."

"I'm curious, Albert. You intend to find where this Gastrothief has taken the people his agents kidnapped and then to call the cavalry, I assume. But how is it that you propose to do that? Do you know where they will strike next? I'm guessing not because if you did you would want to involve the police. You could clear your name and stop the crimes in one fell swoop."

Albert had been quite deliberate in omitting to reveal he had in his possession the phone that Baldwin dropped. He couldn't be certain, but even so he was fairly sure that he would find agents of the Gastrothief in Cornwall. There was a reservation set for tomorrow. A two night stay in the seaside resort of Looe.

He doubted it would be Baldwin attending because Rex had bitten him in the fight last night and left the kind of injury a person couldn't just shake off. It might therefore not be Tanya either as the two appeared to work as a couple. Maybe they were a couple, Albert mused.

The point was that he knew precisely where agents of the Gastrothief were due to be in two days' time. That plan could have changed because of the events in Whitstable and how close he came to catching them – Albert wouldn't know until he got there.

Of course, the question now was whether he was going to be allowed to go anywhere at all. That Mike Atwell hadn't already arrested him was a good sign. He wanted to talk – to hear Albert's side of the story, and Albert wanted to know why.

Instead of answering Mike's question, he posed one of his own. "Are you going to arrest me?"

Mike frowned. "I haven't decided," he replied after a few seconds. "I'm inclined to believe every word you have said."

Albert drilled into Mike's eyes. "You will get into a lot of trouble." He wanted the detective to walk away and pretend he'd never seen Albert Smith, but it was the sort of thing that ended at a disciplinary hearing and could result in a chap losing his pension.

To Albert's surprise, the man sitting opposite just shrugged.

"The person behind your arrest warrant is an idiot," Mike offered an opinion Albert felt inclined to agree with. "Chief Inspector Quinn's sole focus is on the next rung up the ladder. Who he has to step on to get there is of no great concern. He ignores minor cases, handing them down to more junior officers so he can take the big ones, the ones that will get his name in the papers. He wants to arrest you so he can be seen to be actively pursuing whoever was behind the explosion in Whitstable. His track record is one of success because, despite it all, he is clever enough to make sure his teams are filled with people who are far brighter than he is. They solve the crimes; he takes the credit."

Albert remembered men like that when he was still serving. They never seemed to get all that far before their lack of ability was identified.

Mike said, "I have another question for you."

cherry bomb

"*H*ey, wait up!"

Rex and Buster turned their heads to see who was barking at them.

"*I've only got little legs,*" barked a miniature dachshund as it ran to catch up.

She had been with the pack supporting Cerberus, hanging around at the back. Why was she chasing after them now?

Mindy heard the sausage dog too and stopped to let it catch up when Buster and Rex decided they were stopping.

"*Hey, guys.*" The Dachshund bounded up to them. "*I'm Lila. You're trying to find Ernie, right? Did I hear that you were a police dog?*"

Rex said, "*Yes. I was. And yes, the plan is to find the missing dog. Someone has to.*"

"*I'm Devil Dog,*" rasped Buster.

Rex rolled his eyes. "*Dude, you have got to drop the superhero dog thing.*"

Ignoring him, Buster rasped, "*The darkness fears me.*"

Lila, her eyes wide, said, "*That's. So. Cooool. I always wanted to have a superhero name.*"

In his Devil Dog voice, Buster rasped, "*You have to earn it, but if you are here to help us, you can be Cherry Bomb.*"

"*Cherry Bomb,*" Lila repeated, her voice filled with excited wonder.

Rex said, "*Good grief.*"

"*Because you are small, but explosive,*" rasped Buster.

Mindy gave a slight tug on Buster's lead to get his attention.

"*What are you lot saying?*" she asked, knowing she wasn't going to get an answer and wouldn't understand it even if she did. The envy she felt for her aunt's ability had been instant and constant since she discovered it. The dogs were clearly communicating, though much of it appeared to be in movements and with their eyes.

Rex used a back leg to scratch his head. When he finished, he forced his way into the daft conversation still passing between Devil Dog and the newly named Cherry Bomb.

"Hey! If you can stop fantasising about kennels that transform into armoured cars for a moment, we have a missing dog to find."

Buster and Lila looked his way.

"Damned right we do," rasped Devil Dog. *"What can you tell us, Cherry Bomb?"*

"Why are you here anyway?" Rex interrupted before she could answer. *"Why aren't you with Cerberus? I thought he was the king around here."*

"Ha!" spat Lila. *"He likes to think he is. He's won best in breed at Crufts three times and almost won the whole show a year ago. All the other dogs look at him like he's a god."*

"Except you," Rex stated the obvious.

Lila snarled, *"He makes fun of me. Of my size. And my shape,"* she added. *"It's not just me though, he picks on almost everyone, finding something about them to highlight and diminish. It makes the other dogs fight for his attention – they all want to be seen in his inner circle. That's what I was doing when you showed up,"* she admitted, shame clear in her voice. *"Anyway, he hates Ernie. He hates all small dogs. It's only because I am part of the hound group that I get permitted to tag along. He wants to stop you and anyone else from finding Ernie. You needn't worry about him though, whatever he has planned won't succeed."*

"Why's that?" asked Buster.

"Because he's as thick as two short planks."

Rex sniggered at the dachshund's comment. *"Ok, regardless of what Cerberus and his crew do, the dog is missing. In theory I can track him, but I don't have a scent to track."*

"I can take you to his room," offered Buster. *"You can pick it up there."* He started walking, Mindy following behind when his lead went taut again.

The dogs were heading back toward the hotel again, Mindy observed. Checking her watch, she had been trailing around behind Buster, inexplicably collecting additional dogs for over an hour. She believed Aunt Felicity would call her if she was needed elsewhere, yet had to question whether all her tasks were being covered and if this was, in fact, the best use of her time.

Passing a row of cars close to the hotel entrance, Mindy's feet ground to a halt and her jaw dropped open.

Forced to also stop, Buster twisted his body around to see what Mindy was doing.

Mindy didn't know for certain, but if the number plate she was looking at belonged to anyone else, then she was going to be shocked.

She snapped a shot of it and thumbed the button to call her employer.

Accusations and Dates

I was struggling to figure out what to do. Justin was tackling as much as he could, doing his best to make sure the wedding stayed on track. The replacement steak and lobster were coming, and I knew Chef O'Malley would pull off a miracle even though she would make it sound impossible.

As weddings go, especially when considering my recent run of luck, this one was ticking along smoothly. The only real hurdle I faced was the missing dog. Obviously, I was concerned for the poor little fellow, but if he wasn't found by three o'clock when the ceremony was due to start, could I convince the bride to go through with it anyway? I was going to try, that was for certain.

Vince was going to help, and that took some pressure off me. Who knows, maybe Vince would come through for me and find Ernie in time. It wouldn't shock me if he did, and he was far better at snooping around than I was.

Standing in the corridor outside Mr and Mrs Moscovitch's room, I was running through a mental list of all the things I needed to do when my phone rang.

Mindy started talking the moment I connected the call. "Auntie, you're not going to believe this."

Vince made an impressed face when I employed a string of swear-words.

Philippe said, "Wow," in an awe inspired kind of way, like I had just gained some street cred points in his eyes.

"Yes, that's her number plate," I snarled through gritted teeth. Flicking my eyes at Vince, I started to walk, my footsteps fast as I told him, "Don't worry about looking for the dog, I know precisely who's taken him."

"You do?" he questioned.

To Mindy I said, "Stay there, I'll be right down."

Slamming my phone back into my handbag, I could feel a mad darkness descending in my head. Primrose Green's car was here and that had to mean she was too. She was supposed to be at the Hughes wedding in Canterbury, one of her biggest of the year, and yet she was here and there could only be one reason for it – she was messing with my business again.

I'd only recently caught her trying to scare me out of my office by employing a fake ghost. Storming into her office to confront her on the matter ought to have ended it, but the madwoman chose instead to hand over the management of her own event to disrupt mine. She had put the dye in the meat and lobster, and she had taken Ernie.

By the time I reached the hotel lobby I had a full head of steam and was ready to kill. Unable to contain myself when I saw her, I caught the attention of everyone within earshot when I screeched her name.

"Primrose Green, you evil cow!"

I stomped across the lobby, heading for the bar where she was sitting with her shapely legs crossed on a barstool. She had a book in her hand, and a half-finished glass of sparkling wine on the bar by her left elbow. Dressed for a wedding, she wore a cream and white fitted dress with matching heels. A wide-brimmed hat perched atop her handbag on the barstool next to her.

She looked up at my shout, as did everyone else around me, and smiled a broad and confident smile. She looked like the cat who got the cream and all I wanted in the world was to slap it off her face.

"Steady now, Felicity," Vince coached as he hurried along beside me. "You don't know it was her."

"Of course it was her," I snapped, refusing to take my eyes off her as I powered through the bar.

Mindy had been hanging around by the doors – oddly she had three dogs with her now. I could find out what that was about later. She'd seen me and was following, her path aiming to converge with mine near the bar.

Hotel staff from the reception desk were hurrying after me; my scream of insult too loud to ignore. They were probably worried I was about to start a fight.

I wasn't. I wouldn't stoop to that, but I might throw a drink in her face. A brandy perhaps and then ask if anyone around me had a match.

"Hello, Felicity," Primrose smiled again as I drew near. "Is there something the matter?"

"Where is he?" I demanded.

She made a confused face and said, "Who are we talking about?"

Her response was as easy to anticipate as it was stupid.

"The dog, Primrose, the dog. What kind of madness goes through your head that you will steal a bride's dog on the day of her wedding? The poor girl is distraught." I jabbed a finger at her and found a smile of my own. "There will be an arrest, you know. I'll be pressing charges even if the family doesn't. You destroyed thousands of pounds worth of food with your stupid dye. This will end your hopes for the royal wedding, Primrose."

I was expecting her to look embarrassed, or worried, or ... something. Her face was portraying none of those emotions though and when I mentioned the royal wedding, she tipped her head back and laughed.

"Oh, oh that's priceless, Felicity. You think I would stoop to ruining food and what was the other one? Taking the bride's dog? Why would I want to do any of those things?"

Buster's voice arrived in my head. *"She doesn't smell of Ernie. She doesn't smell of dog at all."*

"Is there something I can help with, Mrs Philips?" The question was asked by August Bartram, the hotel manager, who had just arrived by my side.

"This woman took Donna Moscovitch's dog and she's the one who put dye in the food earlier," I accused Primrose directly.

Primrose smiled at the hotel manager. "Hello, August. How are you? Life treating you well? How are your children, Tommy and little Margot? Perhaps you can tell this raving lunatic that I only walked through the hotel doors ten minutes ago."

Of course she knew him; Primrose undoubtedly had weddings here herself just as often as I did.

"So you got someone to do it for you," I sneered, ignoring her pathetic attempt to develop an alibi. "You're still behind it. You're the only one with motive."

Primrose scoffed, "What motive? You think I need to scupper your weddings? You seem to do a good enough job on your own. How many of the couples you were set to marry this year actually made it down the aisle?"

It was a cruel barb because it was true. This season had been terrible for me and each of my recent dramas had made the news because they involved celebrities or public figures.

Through a clenched jaw I demanded, "Just tell me where he is, Primrose. Give me back the dog for goodness sake. Be decent for once."

Primrose shook her head in despair and turned away from me.

"August I've had quite enough of this woman's accusations. There is nothing to substantiate any of her claims. She recently tried to accuse me of murder, of all things and she still hasn't apologised for it."

Mindy touched my arm. "Perhaps we should go, Auntie."

August agreed, speaking quietly when he leaned in to say. "I must ask that you desist, Mrs Philips. Unless you have some evidence that implicates Mrs Green ..."

I had nothing. To me her very presence was enough to prove she had to be behind it and a question burst from my lips.

"If you're not here to ruin this wedding, Primrose, why are you here?"

Primrose had her book in her right hand and her glass of sparkling wine in the left. She was happily paying me no attention already, treating me like I was an annoyance that would go away by itself.

However, she twisted around on her seat once more to look in my eyes when she answered.

"To tell you now would spoil the surprise, Felicity. I think I shall wait until later."

There was something about the confident tone she employed, something that zipped down my spine like ice water. She had something up her sleeve and whatever it was, I felt certain I wasn't going to like it.

Before the hotel manager felt a need to repeat his request, and so that I wouldn't damage my relationship with him or the hotel where I hoped to have many more weddings in the future, I turned around and walked away.

Exhaling slowly as I attempted to calm myself, I aimed for a quiet corner of the hotel's lobby. I needed to gather myself, but I also wanted to quiz Buster about what he had been able to discover and who the new dogs were. I couldn't do that until I got rid of August.

Massaging my forehead and looking suitably apologetic, I said, "I'm sorry, August. Despite what Primrose says, she is guilty. I will prove it, but I shouldn't have caused a scene the way I did."

August accepted what I had to say, but warned, "I trust there will be no further incidents, Felicity."

"No, August. When I find the evidence I need, I will bring it to you first. The police will need to attend, but we can do that quietly."

"Hmm, yes, the police," he commented. He would not have enjoyed having a host of squad cars and officers descending on his place of work a few hours ago. He wouldn't hold me to blame for that (I hoped) even though it was my bride and her family who placed the call. Having them back again was something he would wish to be managed carefully.

I made a further promise to leave Primrose alone until I could prove she was behind Ernie's disappearance and let the hotel manager get on with his day.

The moment he was out of range to hear what I was saying, I whipped my head around to look up into Vince's eyes and grabbed his lapels with both hands.

Mindy, Philippe, and most especially Vince made shocked faces.

"You said that you were in love with me," I reminded Vince.

"I was concussed, if you remember," he replied carefully, clearly wondering what might be coming next. "But yes, I admit that I am infatuated with you and will very happily become your significant other. You have been playing rather hard to get so far."

"Well, Mr Slater, here is your chance to prove yourself. If you want me, find out what Primrose Green did with Donna Moscovitch's champion Pomeranian."

Vince's eyes dilated. "I find the dog and I get ... you."

"Yes." I nodded.

Mindy gripped Philippe's arm and started to drag him away. "I feel a need to check on the plants on this side of the room," she declared in an overly loud fashion. "Come and help me, Philippe."

I blinked, rerunning my words through my head.

"Wait, no, I don't mean ..."

"Uh-uh," Vince shot me his shark-infested smile. "A deal is a deal. I find the dog and I get to *have* you."

My cheeks were so bright red and hot I thought they might catch fire.

"That's not what I meant at all."

"But it is what you said," Mindy called over her shoulder as she pretended to inspect the hotel's house plants.

"A date," I offered. "I was talking about a date. A proper one. It could even involve kissing," I hedged even though I really wasn't sure I was ready to be kissing him. Not that kissing was a big deal, it was what it led to that had me freaking out.

Vince narrowed his eyes. "Ten dates."

"Two," I countered immediately.

"Ten."

"Three then."

"Ten, Felicity. Ten dates is enough time for me to prove to you who I am and to convince you to trust me. Saving your life didn't do the trick and how about this: I won't even try to get you into bed. We can go on ten dates, each of which I will pay for and at the end of them, if you don't want to explore our relationship further, I will shake your hand and walk away. I'll even take the bug out of your phone I've been using to track your location."

I blurted out, "What!"

He grinned again. "Only joking."

I pressed my lips together and squinted up at him. He was a pirate in a hand-cut suit, but he was nice to look at and he kept himself in shape. He even had his own money and if it ever got that far, I'd seen him naked and … well, let's just say I knew I wouldn't be disappointed on the wedding night. Not that we were ever going to get married, you understand.

Ten dates.

In the middle of all the chaos and drama of the day, I somehow found myself with a boyfriend. Even if he was a temporary one.

I stepped back and offered him my right hand.

"Ten dates."

He smiled like he'd just won the lottery and rubbed his hands together in gleeful anticipation. We shook on it, and I got the feeling I'd just swum inside a cave and was soon to discover it was in fact the mouth of a giant shark.

I didn't get to dwell on it for very long because a new drama was breaking out in the lobby.

THE EX-BOYFRIEND

An argument had broken out, and though I couldn't see who all the protagonists were, I heard Denise when she raised her voice.

"No! No, Angus, you cannot be here!" she gasped in horror.

Coming closer, I could see she was blocking him with her body, her arms out to prevent him from passing though he was trying to dodge around her. Denise's boyfriend, the one Mindy took a fancy to, was with her, but was taking no part. If anything, he looked unconcerned about her panic.

"You have to go!" she added. "Donna is marrying Damien."

Angus was shouting when he replied, "But she doesn't want to!" Then he was waving something in her face, and it took me a moment to spot that it was his phone. "Read this!" he demanded, thrusting it at her.

Denise's boyfriend continued to look bored and had backed a yard away from the situation. Spotting me heading his way with my entourage, he considered himself unneeded and crossed the lobby.

"Denise, can I be of assistance?" I asked, striding quickly to get to her.

Angus – I knew his name but nothing else – shot angry eyes in my direction.

"This doesn't concern you," he snapped rudely. "This doesn't concern anyone but me and Donna."

Denise hadn't looked around when I spoke to her, and she was still staring down at the phone in her hands. Her expression was one of disbelief.

"You sent this to yourself," she accused Angus, her features shifting to reflect the anger in Angus's face.

He screwed up his face, showing how ridiculous he thought her remark was.

"It's from her number," he pointed out. "How did I manage to pull that off? I'm going up to see her, right now."

"No, you're not!" argued Denise, raising her voice.

August left the reception desk and stepped in.

"Please, ladies and gentlemen. I must insist that you keep your conversation to a respectful volume and move away from the hotel lobby.

This is not the place to have an argument. Can I offer you one of our anterooms so your ... discussion can be made in private?"

Angus's voice was dangerous when he said, "The only place I'm going is Donna's room. Tell me where she is."

I wasn't going to stay quiet any longer, and whoever the young man was, I certainly didn't want him going anywhere near my bride.

"Angus, my name is Felicity. I am the wedding planner. I'm afraid you are not going to be permitted to see Donna unless she expressly insists that she wishes to. Even then, I need you to calm down first." He was going to argue, but a firm index finger held in the air between us proved sufficient to gave him pause while I addressed Denise. "Denise, what is this about?"

"Donna doesn't want to marry that wet fish, Damien," Angus interjected before Denise could answer. "She wants me."

Behind me, Mindy murmured, "This is better than TV."

I shot her a warning glance and in so doing noticed that Philippe had wandered away and was now on the other side of the lobby conversing with Hudson.

"She doesn't want you," Denise refused to believe what Angus was saying. "She's marrying Damien."

Angus laughed. "You keep saying that, but you've read the message she sent me."

Denise might have, but I hadn't.

"May I?" I requested, holding my hand out for Denise to pass the phone she still held. She pushed it into my palm, and I touched the screen, bringing it to life.

Mindy crowded in against my right arm so she could read it too, and Vince came in close behind me to look over my shoulder.

In Vince's case, I think he just wanted to press his body against me, and I struggled to decide if I should jab an elbow into his gut so he backed off a little, or ignore him because he was probably just trying to wind me up.

In the end I was too transfixed by the message to do anything but read it through three times.

'Angus, I've made a terrible mistake! I can't marry Damien! Please come to the hotel and find me. I never should have split up with you.'

I took out my own phone to confirm the number it came from was the same one I had listed for Donna.

It was.

The timestamp on it was less than three hours ago – the bride had sent it after she discovered her dog was missing. It made no sense. So far as I knew, Donna had been dating Damien for more than a year and she seemed utterly besotted by him.

My head snapped up when Denise swore.

"What's he doing here?" barked Damien, coming into the hotel lobby with his groomsmen in tow.

I shoved the phone back into Denise's hand and twisted my arm to grab Vince's sleeve. I didn't even need to say anything – Vince was already moving.

"Let's be calm now gentlemen, please." Vince moved around Denise, August, and Angus to place himself between the groom and Donna's ex-boyfriend. Vince is an imposing figure, and his request was enough to give Damien and his friends pause.

Denise let out a small groan and placed a hand to her belly. She looked to be in discomfort but no one else noticed.

Now dominating the lobby, as more people here to attend the wedding felt drawn to the unfolding drama, August was desperate to shift us.

He spoke politely but sternly, "Please, I must insist that we move to a side room," but no one was listening because Angus had snatched his phone back from Denise and was offering it to Damien.

"Here," he goaded. "Read it for yourself. You're out, mate." His confident words were met with surly glares from the groomsmen and a confused, if angry expression from the groom himself.

"What?" snapped Damien. "What's this rubbish?"

He took the phone and there was nothing I could do to stop him from reading it. He was going to find out what Donna wrote no matter what because Angus would tell him if he didn't see it for himself.

Gripping Mindy's arm, I said, "Go get dressed, Mindy. I need you to take over for me. I need to focus on getting this wedding back on track.

If I can," I added, feeling less than hopeful – this was a real spanner in the works. "Take Phillipe, team up with Justin, rope in some hotel staff, and get everything done. I'll check in on you as soon as I can."

Mindy's face was doubtful. "You really think this wedding is going ahead, Auntie?"

I nodded my head. I couldn't blame Primrose for this latest problem. At least, I didn't think I could. Regardless, until Donna boldly stated that she didn't want to marry Damien, I was going to proceed as if the ceremony was going ahead. I was being paid for it after all.

When I said that to Mindy, she asked, "What about Ernie? Do I put Buster back in your room and hope he turns up?"

"*No*," rasped Buster in his silly Devil Dog voice. "*You turn me loose and trust me to find him with my sidekicks Cherry Bomb and ...*" Buster made a thoughtful face while glancing at the German Shepherd. "*Blood Tooth?*"

The German Shepherd twisted his head to look at Buster side on and I watched as he exchanged a glance with the dachshund. I couldn't hear if he was saying anything, but to me it looked as if the other dogs were trying to figure out what was going on. Buster was talking to me, and I was answering – they were pulling the same sort of faces I might if I saw a fish applying for an accountancy job.

"*Yeah, I'll explain in a minute,*" Buster spoke to the other dogs in a dismissive manner. Looking up at me and wagging his tail, he asked, "*How about it?*"

A few yards away, with Vince doing his best to keep Damien and Angus apart, a full-scale fight looked to be moments away. I had no time to deliberate.

Quickly, I crouched, to unclip the lead from Buster's collar.

"Now, you promise to be a good boy and not cause havoc?" I implored him. I had enough trouble without August calling me to report my dog had just trashed the dining room or something.

Buster's response was instant. "*Scout's honour.*"

"You're a dog, Buster. You weren't in the scouts. Just ... behave for me, please. And if you can find Ernie, bring him to the bridal suite as fast as you can." I was about to get up when I found I simply had to ask, "Who are your new friends?"

Buster blinked. "*I just introduced them.*"

"No, I mean, where are their owners? Where did they come from?"

It was clear to me that Buster was conversing with the other two dogs in between talking to me as I was getting his half of the conversation. I was sure they were answering, though of course I couldn't hear their thoughts the way I could his.

"*Well, Lila says her human is outside somewhere probably going nuts because she wandered off and didn't come back. And Rex is on the run from the police and a mysterious gang of organised criminals and is hiding out here with his human until the coast is clear.*"

I never knew what to believe when it came to Buster. I loved the daft mutt, but he lived in a parallel universe half the time.

Rising from my crouch, I sent Mindy on her way, telling her to hurry, and gave Buster permission to do what he could to find Ernie. The three dogs sauntered around the loud and unruly mob of humanity blocking the hotel lobby and waited at the hotel doors, wagging their tails until the next human along opened it to come in and found themselves forced to jump out of the way as the canine crew bounded outside.

The argument between Angus and Damien had reached fever pitch, but it was August whose voice rang out the loudest.

"Enough!" he roared, silencing everyone. "This hotel and its staff will not tolerate this kind of behaviour!"

I stepped in to support him, but he had more to say.

"Either this dispute is resolved with the bride right now, or *I* myself will call off the wedding."

Vince moved Angus back, separating him from Damien and his groomsmen, not that their attempts to intimidate Angus were having any effect.

I was about to suggest we all went calmly and quietly up to the bridal suite, but before I could, Denise let out a wail she was trying hard to suppress and clutched at her stomach.

"I don't feel well," she hissed between gritted teeth. There were beads of sweat on her forehead, and she was looking pale. "I think I might have been poisoned."

ACCUSATIONS

Denise looked to be in some pain, and I was going to ask what I could do, planning to escort her to a seat when her eyes widened in stark panic, and she bolted for the nearest ladies' restroom.

I looked around as the restroom door slammed - I was surrounded by men. I was quite actually the only woman in sight.

Sighing as I set out to face yet another problem, I twisted around to face the groom as I started toward the toilets.

"Damien, I know you want to speak with Donna; can you give me a minute?"

"A minute?" he gawped at me. "No, I can't, Mrs Philips. I need to see Donna right now!"

"So do I," agreed Angus, generating a fresh exchange of threats and insults.

Vince was looking my way, and as I reached the restroom door and shoved it open, I used my eyes to implore him for help. Pausing in the doorway, I hoped he might give me a reason to believe he was going to do something, but all I got was a cheeky wink.

Muttering under my breath and moving as fast as I could because Angus was running for the stairs just as Damien and his groomsmen dived into an elevator, I kicked the door fully open and shouted, "Denise are you okay?"

"Go away!" she replied in a horrified voice. "I think someone put laxatives in the champagne. It's all I've had since breakfast." It sounded as though she was straining every muscle in her body to fight the inevitable and with a rush of realisation, I ducked back out the door with a final, "I'm going up to the bridal suite. I'll check on you later."

She wanted me out of the restroom because she was about to fill it with unspeakable noises.

Back in the lobby the elevator doors were still open, but only because Vince was holding them. Damien and his friends were a little upset about this, or so I judged from the language they were employing.

Had Vince not looked like a retired heavyweight boxer, I suspect they might have attempted to remove him by force. Instead, they stuck to insults about his parentage and sexual preferences – not that I believed anyone was prepared to do with a goat what they were suggesting Vince saw as a weekend hobby.

I ran across the lobby, August watching me with a worrying lack of sympathy as I ducked under Vince's arm and into the elevator.

There was no way we were going to get to the bridal suite before Angus, and Damien was most displeased about it.

"You are supposed to be on my side, Felicity," he grumbled, his forehead creased by his angry grimace. "What else am I paying you for?"

"Be polite now, there's a good chap," warned Vince.

I didn't need a protector, and though in other circumstances I might rather like it, today, having been coerced into a series of dates that quite frankly terrified me, Vince's desire to rush to my defence was unwelcome.

So were Damien's comments, though I was more than capable of responding to them myself.

"To the best of my knowledge, Damien, you are not paying me at all. Donna's parents are picking up the bill. Is that not the case?" I invited him to challenge me, and he fell silent. I knew it wouldn't last long before he found something new to say, but of course the elevator had completed its journey and with a ping the doors opened.

Damien barged through them, rudely clipping my shoulder in his desperation. The groomsmen were right on his heels, and I let them go, following at my own pace with Vince by my side.

The bridal suite was just around the corner, the sound of the groom and groomsmens' running feet echoing along the corridor as they raced to get there. Like me, they could hear Angus and he was shouting.

"But you sent me this message!" His voice filled the air with indignant disbelief. "Don't tell me that you didn't."

My pace was quick; I didn't want to run, but I was hurrying, and Donna's reply only made me go faster.

"I didn't send it, Angus! I've got no idea why you would think that I would."

I turned the corner just in time to see Damien and his groomsmen arrive at the door to the bridal suite. Surprisingly, Angus was in the corridor - I had expected him to be inside the bridal suite. It was Mr Moscovitch who was barring Angus's entrance, and unfortunately that made him an easy target for the four men running straight at him.

Without Vince there to intervene, Damien threw himself bodily at his love rival.

Vince started running. "I'll split them up," he assured me as he accelerated.

All I could do was throw my hands in the air. The groom and his groomsmen were all wearing their morning suits. There was no need for them to be dressed this early, but I saw this all the time. Wanting to get to the bar for a couple of drinks before the event and already in a celebratory mood, the men in the wedding party tended to don their outfits well in advance.

When I heard a rip of material, I lied to myself it had probably come from Angus and not the groom.

Mr Moscovitch was trying to separate the two men who were now rolling around on the carpet in the corridor outside the bridal suite.

Screeching like a banshee, Mrs Moscovitch, accompanied by the bride herself, tried to get involved.

The scene was one of utter bedlam. Angus and Damien were throwing fists and feet and rolling around like two particularly energetic lovers as each fought to get the dominant position. The groomsmen found themselves in two distinct camps, one of them clearly intending to wallop Angus if he could find an opening, while the other two attempted to restrain him.

Donna was sobbing uncontrollably again, Mrs Moscovitch was demanding her husband 'do something' and I was rather worried what the gangster might choose to do if given free rein.

Vince arrived at the scene of the fight, and whatever else I might say or think about him, he knows how to deal with aggressive situations. Stepping over the two combatants, he gripped their collars and yanked both men apart.

Angus and Damien continued trying to thrash at each other, a stray kick swinging towards Vince's soft parts until he blocked it with an efficient and practised move.

"That's enough now," Vince growled in a tone that suggested little more nonsense would be tolerated. Holding a fistful of the groom's jacket in his giant left mitt, Vince thrust Damien towards the bride's father, and lifting Angus to his feet, walked him in the opposite direction.

Both men were seething, their eyes filled with murder as they glared at each other, but a distraction soon came in the form of Donna as she raced to Damien's side.

"Babe are you okay? Oh, my goodness you're hurt!" she exclaimed with a gasp, one hand rising to cover her mouth.

She was right too, the groom had blood coming from his nose, a fat lip, and what looked like the beginnings of a black eye forming. Not only that, the right shoulder of his morning suit was torn open.

Overwhelmed with emotion, Damien shoved his bride away and snarled into her face.

"So you don't want to marry me, eh?" he spat. "Yes, I've seen the message you sent him. Well, he's welcome to you if that's the case!"

Donna's sobbing had momentarily ceased through her concern for the groom, but it was back now with a vengeance.

"No!" she wailed. "I haven't done anything! I haven't sent him any messages. I don't want anything to do with him. I love you, Damien."

"That's not what this message says," interrupted Angus, unwilling to be denied his opportunity to speak.

"I didn't send it!" Donna screamed at him.

Angus was going to argue, but it was Damien who got in first. "Then who did?" he was challenging his bride and making it very clear that he did not believe her.

I wanted to say something, but for the life of me I had no idea what I could do at this juncture to alter the trajectory of this wedding. You might think that I shouldn't care too much so long as I get paid, but that has never been the way I operate. What I want is to go home at the end of a successful wedding knowing that the happy couple and all of the guests had the most amazing time possible. Was there any chance that that could still happen today?

Once again Donna attempted to defend herself. "I don't know, darling," she begged Damien to listen. "Anyone could have gotten hold of my phone and sent a text message."

"Really?" Damien sneered. "What was his number even doing in your phone?"

"It wasn't in my phone," Donna snapped back without needing to think of her reply

"So, you just happened to remember it, did you?" Damien was not going to be easily convinced. "Angus's digits are so precious that you memorised them. Is that the case?"

Donna was so confused and distraught she could barely speak. Between sobs that shook her shoulders, she managed to cry, "No. Why would you think any of this is true. We are supposed to be getting married today."

"In less than two hours," pointed out Mrs Moscovitch.

"I love you," Donna insisted, looking up at her groom with hurt filled eyes. "Why won't you believe me?"

Damien looked to be struggling to decide what to say or do or believe. His wedding day was not going according to plan, but did he really want to throw the whole thing away?

Afforded a few moments of silence where none of the protagonists were saying anything, I stepped in.

"Angus, before you received this message, when was the last time you heard from Donna?"

All eyes swung his way to hear the answer.

Reluctantly, he admitted, "We split up more than a year ago. I haven't heard from her since about a week after that."

"What was the nature of your last communication?" I pressed him to answer, hoping that I had guessed correctly.

Angus no longer looked angry. Mostly, he looked like he knew he had lost.

Shrugging one shoulder in a defeated manner, he said, "I called her wanting to get back together and she told me it was never going to happen."

"And you haven't heard from her since that day until you got this message an hour ago?"

Angus exhaled a weary sigh. "I messaged her a few times and she never answered."

I swung my gaze away from him to look directly at the groom. The message in my eyes was a very simple one and mercifully I did not need to push him any harder than that.

Reaching out, Damien pulled Donna into his arms and held her against his chest. He was whispering something, an apology I felt certain, that the rest of us could not hear. That was as it should be.

Someone had played a cruel trick and it had to be someone who knew the bride very well. Well enough to know there was a former boyfriend still in love with her and who could be manipulated. It was another blow to a day that was supposed to be perfect for the happy couple.

It did, however, and much to my surprise, create the conditions required to solve another problem.

"We haven't been able to locate Ernie yet," Damien explained, his voice full of apology. "I'm sorry, Donna. We're not giving up, but I want to know if you will go through with the ceremony anyway?" He didn't give her a chance to answer, possibly expecting her to start crying again and refuse. Instead, he ploughed on, adding weight to his argument. "I don't know who could have taken him, but if they did it in an attempt to stop the ceremony, we cannot let them win. Will you Donna? Will you marry me today?"

No one spoke, all eyes in the corridor aimed directly at the bride and groom, as with bated breath we waited for Donna to answer.

She was tearful which was exactly what I expected, but inside I was cheering when she said, "Yes, Damien, I will."

Looking dejected, and watching the bride and groom embrace, Angus turned away. Vince placed a comradely hand upon his shoulder, just for a second, and murmured something to which Angus nodded.

Whatever Vince's words of wisdom might have been they caused Donna's rejected former boyfriend to offer a parting comment.

"I'm sorry for the mess I've caused today," Angus tried to find the right words even if his heart wasn't in them. "I guess someone played a trick on me. I wish you both luck." He turned away again and a few moments later he vanished from sight around the corner.

So that was the relationship drama dealt with, but I still had someone who was going out of their way to mess with this wedding. The food had been ruined, the bride's little dog was still missing, Mr Moscovitch was up to something, and with a jolt of recollection, I added Denise's poisoning to the list.

Blurting out the words, I asked Donna, "Have you had any of the champagne your sister was drinking?"

She lifted her head away from Damien's chest. Her eyes when they met mine were the most miserable I had ever seen on a bride in my entire career and though none of it was my fault I felt an overwhelming need to make her pain go away.

Donna gave a slight shake of her head. "No. I don't really like champagne. Ellie and the girls polished it off."

The bridesmaids!

Given how poorly Denise was when I left her, and her claim that the poison must have been in the champagne ... well, let's just say I was running again.

STRANGE SECRETS

At the door when they were waiting to go outside, Rex looked down at Buster. *"You feel like explaining what we just saw?"*

Buster sniggered, and when the door opened, he bounded outside without offering an answer.

"Hey, wait up," barked Lila, rushing to keep up.

Rex let the bulldog get away from the front of the hotel, but once they were on the grass, he got in front of him and forced Buster to stop.

"Come on. Spill," he demanded.

Lila trotted around Buster so she was facing him too. *"Yeah, what was that? You were talking to your human, and she answered. How did you do that?"*

Buster lowered his back end onto the grass. There were very few animals who knew about his human's unique skill, and it wasn't so much that he tried to keep it quiet, more that Felicity tried her best to only talk to him when they were alone.

That wasn't always possible, of course, as today had shown.

"She can understand me," he told the two dogs. *"Don't ask me how, and it's just her, no one else."*

Lila couldn't believe her ears. *"That is beyond bizarre."*

Rex couldn't help but doubt the bulldog's claim. *"Your human can understand you?"*

"Not just me," Buster explained. *"Felicity can hear the cat too."*

"You're serious?" Lila found herself vacillating between outright disbelief and unparalleled excitement.

"She can't hear anyone else though. Not so far, at least, and she couldn't hear us when we first moved in with her. It started a couple of weeks later."

Unable to shift the doubt, Rex chose to leave the subject for now and test it out later. To him it seemed more likely that what he'd just witnessed was a quirk of good timing; the bulldog's human supplying an answer that made it sound like she'd understood what Buster said.

Dismissing it for now, Rex said, *"I still need to sample the Pomeranian's scent. Can you help me with that?"*

"*Why don't we just get him to ask the humans?*" asked Lila, sniggering at her own joke.

Buster frowned. "*Because its only Felicity who can hear me and she doesn't know where Ernie is,*" he pointed out, Lila's joke going straight over his head. "*Honestly, Cherry Bomb, if you want to be a superhero sidekick, you need to pay more attention.*"

Before Lila could respond, Rex butted in, "*Can we get on with the task in hand? I need you to take me to somewhere I will be able to identify Ernie's scent. Can you do that?*" Rex's desire to get the show moving was unambiguous and his tone made that abundantly clear.

"*All right, all right,*" Buster set off, aiming to skirt the hotel, and come back in through the patio on the other side. "*Keep your fur on.*"

"*Where are we going?*" asked Lila, trotting along beside the bulldog.

Buster flicked his head back to the main doors. "*There's too much human traffic that way. Someone will intercept us, wondering where our humans are, and that will just slow us down. We need to get up to the bridal suite; that's where Ernie was hanging out. We can all get a fresh sense of his scent there.*"

Glad to be on the hunt, Rex encouraged the other two to quicken their pace; he wanted to get on with it. He wasn't overly bothered about defeating the Doberman or not - he was quite happy to ignore the idiot. However, he could not deny that beating the Doberman just as he said he would held a certain appeal.

Little did the three dogs know that they were being watched by not one but two interested parties.

142

UNDECIDED. ON MORE THAN ONE COUNT

Albert rose from his chair and extended his hand to be shaken by Mike Atwell. The serving Detective Sergeant had a good grip; something Albert used as a measure of a person. To Albert's mind a weak handshake suggested a person with questionable integrity.

"You realise, of course, that I'm going to have to accompany you while we look for your dog," Mike made it very clear that while he believed what Albert was telling him, he was as yet undecided about what course of action he should take.

In truth, though he was yet to admit it to anyone, Mike had a plan for his future, and it did not include arresting Albert Smith. He wanted to know more about this supposed Gastrothief and Albert's investigation into the spree of associated crimes. So, while Mike wanted to continue picking Albert's brains on the subject, he nevertheless accepted that what Albert wanted and arguably needed to do, was find his dog who was loose somewhere on the grounds.

In the hotel lobby, Albert asked at reception and was advised that a large German Shepherd had only recently left the premises using the front door.

Confused, Albert attempted to confirm what he was hearing. "I'm sorry, you said he was with a bulldog and a dachshund?"

"Yes, that's correct," confirmed Elaine, one of the staff currently manning the reception desk. "I believe the bulldog belongs to Felicity Philips."

Albert widened his eyes in a display that indicated he had no idea who Felicity Philips was.

"Oh," frowned Elaine. "Are you not here for the Moscovitch wedding? I thought all the dog owners were part of that event."

Mike leaned in to touch Albert's arm. "I know Felicity Philips. She's a high-end wedding planner."

Elaine smiled. "That's right."

Taking Albert to one side, Mike suggested, "We can look for your dog outside, but if we don't find him there, we can always come back in and track down Felicity. She'll be in the marquee for the event or with the bride or doing something to do with the ceremony and the reception. That lady has a big personality – she won't be hard to find."

Still surprised by how his day was going; Albert was in the company of a senior detective who was under orders to arrest him but choosing not to at the risk of his own career, Albert followed Mike out into the hotel gardens.

Standing on the front steps, which gave the two men an elevated position from which to observe the surrounding gardens, there were plenty of dogs to see, but no sign of Rex or the bulldog Albert now knew to look for.

Huffing, and wishing, not for the first time, that Rex had a recall device fitted to his head, Albert turned right and set off to look for his dog. He couldn't have known it, but he set off in the absolute opposite direction to the one he wanted.

BRIDESMAIDS IN DISTRESS

Questions followed me down the corridor as I ran to get to the bridesmaids' rooms. That the bridesmaids were no longer in the bridal suite had been obvious the moment Donna burst from it with her parents - Ellie, Christy, and Juniper would not have stayed inside with so much drama unfolding. At the time, my guess had been that they were giving themselves some quiet time to get their dresses on.

Remembering Denise in the ladies' restroom, I now prayed that was the case. We were t-minus ... I checked my watch and swore because we were down to under a hundred minutes before the Wedding March was due to start playing.

Knowing this industry as well as I do, I had placed the three brides-maids a short distance from the bridal suite and around a corner. None of Donna's three friends had a man accompanying them to the event which meant one of two things: they were either single, or they were planning to act as if they were single.

I do not sit in judgement, and I know well enough how many hotel beds go unslept in once the alcohol begins flowing at the reception and single persons somehow buoyed along by the romance of the occasion find themselves drawn to each other.

Accepting that I had to provide a reason for my behaviour as well as explain about the Moscovitch's eldest daughter, I stopped running for a moment to explain.

"I believe someone might have slipped something into that bottle of champagne. I left Denise in the ladies' restroom in the hotel lobby." I wafted a hand in front of my general belly area and said, "I believe she was suffering from a little gastric distress. I need to check how the bridesmaids are doing."

Message delivered, I continued on my way, walking backwards in anticipation that there would be more questions coming. However, instead of questions everyone started to follow me.

And they were running.

Around the next corner and opposite the elevator bank, I performed a mental check to be certain I had the right room number and hammered on the door.

"Ellie? Ellie are you in there?" I called out, my face close to the door and one hand on the door handle as I debated whether to call down to reception and ask them to open it for me.

I got no answer, but questioned whether I might have heard something coming from inside the room.

Catching up to me, Donna chose to repeat my shouts, hammering on the door with a raised fist.

"Ellie! Ellie open the door. It's Donna. Are you okay?"

This time I could be certain I heard a response, and though it was muffled, it sounded a lot like, "I can't come to the door."

Seeing how much luck we were having, Damien asked, "Where are the other girls staying?"

Donna answered him before I could.

"Juniper is staying in that one," Donna pointed to the next door along. "And Christy is in the one on the other side of that."

Mr and Mrs Moscovitch, moving slightly slower than their daughter and their soon to be son-in-law, caught up to us and between those two and Damien, they covered the other two doors.

All three of us were calling out to the girls inside but none of them were coming to open the doors.

Vince asked, "Would you like me to open it, dear?"

I turned to find him leaning nonchalantly against the wall behind me. His arms were crossed, and he looked relaxed. When he saw me look his way, his smile turned wolfish. With a flick of his shoulder muscles, he propelled himself away from the wall and was reaching into an inside jacket pocket as he crossed the corridor.

I could hear Mrs Moscovitch on the phone to Denise and that meant Donna's sister was alive at least. Denise said it could have been laxatives in the champagne and that had to be based on the effect they were having. Perhaps the bridesmaids were not in any danger, but they were supposed to be walking down the aisle behind the bride in just over an hour and a half …

I nodded to Vince, giving him my permission to do his thing and stepped out of the way taking Donna with me.

"What's he going to do?" the bride asked, her face scrunched in question as she attempted to peer around Vince's giant frame.

I knew from witnessing it that Vince had learned a few tricks during his time as a security specialist. Opening doors was just one of them. With a click, the door to Ellie's room popped open and Vince stepped back.

"Thank you, Mr Slater," I remarked politely as I went through the door.

I heard him snigger, "You might want to give it a minute," and I was turning to question what he meant when the wall of smell hit me.

Donna gagged and ran back out into the corridor from where she called, "Are you all right, Ellie?"

A plaintive wail emanated from the bathroom, "No! I feel terrible!"

Hiding in the corridor as I willed my feet to ignore the stench so someone could check on the room's occupant, Vince asked, "Shall I open the other doors?"

Trying to breathe through my sleeve, not that it was making much difference, I lifted my face to say, "Yes, please," before burying my face back into the material that was providing the only barrier I had.

Ellie stumbled from the bathroom, gripping the doorframe as if it were the only thing keeping her upright. Her hair and makeup appeared to still be more or less intact, and she was still in her bathrobe, not the bridesmaid dress which I could now see hanging inside a wardrobe door on the other side of the room.

She saw me and let a slow sigh escape her lips.

"Is it just me?" she asked.

Despite the smell, which I was slowly getting used to – not that I wanted to breathe it in – I went to get her, putting one arm around her shoulders and guiding her to sit on the edge of her bed.

"Just take a few deep breaths," I coached. "Is it just your tummy?" I'm not sure why I employed a child's word, but Ellie didn't seem to notice.

She nodded, flopping back onto the bed. "That and I feel like I've been run over by a train. Is it just me?" she repeated her question, probably because she could hear voices echoing in the corridor.

"No. Denise is suffering too, and I think it might be all four of you. Donna said she didn't have the champagne."

Ellie placed a hand on her stomach, panic spreading across her face. A half second of debate followed, after which she bolted for the bathroom again wailing, "How is there anything left in me to come out?"

My heart went out to the poor girl, and I left her to her misery as I went to see if the others were even worse.

They weren't. They were no better either.

Someone had done a number on the bridesmaids and the maid of honour, but who was behind it? It had to be the same person who ruined the food and dognapped Ernie. Someone close to the bride, that was for sure, which ruined my theory that it was Primrose, and I cannot easily express how disappointed that made me.

Mr Moscovitch was skulking in a corner, not really getting involved and not saying anything as usual. On Vince's advice I wasn't going to say anything about what I had seen. He was a seriously dangerous gangster with ties to various organised criminal factions and had escaped the mass arrests that came after Patricia Fisher exposed the Alliance of Families.

He had a gun and was paying dangerous people to do something, but I couldn't see how he could possibly be responsible for ruining his own daughter's wedding. That he doted on her was without question. Dismissing him since I wasn't brave or stupid enough to challenge him about the gun and my worry that he might plan to kill whoever was behind the sabotage, I turned my attention back to the bridesmaids.

Mrs Moscovitch had gone in search of Denise, and I had to pray that all four could recover in time to struggle through the ceremony. Drugs were needed and I used my phone to place a call down to the hotel reception.

"Champneys Resort and Spa. You are speaking to Elaine. How may I help you?"

"Elaine, this is Felicity Philips. I have three ladies suffering from ..." I searched for a polite way of putting it and settled for, "accidental ingestion of a large dose of laxatives." I didn't believe for one moment that there was anything accidental about it, but there was no point introducing that topic of discussion.

I heard Elaine say, "Goodness," and cut her off before she could ask how it happened.

"It's the bridesmaids and I need them up and on their feet in an hour. Can you brief the hotel medic and send whoever that is to rooms 106,108, and 110 as fast as you can?"

"Yes, of course." Someone was talking in the background, distracting Elaine even as I was trying to talk to her. It was a man's voice, but I wasn't expecting Elaine's announcement.

"Um, Mr Bartram wishes to speak with you, Mrs Philips."

The next thing I knew I had August's voice in my ear again.

"Felicity, did I just hear that your bridesmaids are sick?"

"Yes."

I heard August sniff in a thoughtful breath before saying, "We have a licensed doctor working in our spa. I will have him attend them."

A wave of relief washed over me. "Thank you, August. Thank you so much."

He wasn't done though. "I'm afraid I have another problem." He sounded tense and disappointed. My heart sank, guessing that Buster had gone and got himself into trouble. What had he done this time? I was going to apologise in advance, my brain scrambling to concoct a plausible reason for my stupid lump of a dog to be causing chaos when August asked, "Do you know a lady called Virginia Walters?"

I'd been fretting before, thinking my dog might have broken something valuable or taken a poop in the main dining hall, but the hotel manager asking me about my sister froze my heart.

"Is she okay?" I gasped.

scents on the Breeze

B uster led the way, not needing his nose to navigate back to the bridal suite and a good thing too because the entire hotel was awash with overlapping and intertwining dog scents.

Rex was about as focused as he could be, glad to have something interesting to do, and determined that he would employ the skills he knew he possessed to solve a problem that otherwise might escalate.

Where was the missing dog? What had happened to him? And who had taken him? These questions and more were stuck in Rex's head though his friends were more interested in discussing what superpowers they might be able to use in solving the crime.

"How about laser eyeballs?" asked Lila.

Buster grumbled in his Devil Dog voice, *"Too clichéd."*

Lila made a humming noise as she thought. *"Fire breath?"*

"*You'd burn your whiskers off,*" Buster pointed out. "*Could be cool though. How about a utility belt holding exploding gravy bones? We could use them to defeat evil hench dogs.*"

Lila didn't need to consider it for long. "*Nah, I'd be too tempted to eat them.*"

Filtering out the inane babble, Rex closed his eyes and dissected what he could smell. There were twenty-seven individual dog scents, each as different as the colours of the rainbow to Rex's nose. Of them, he could identify nineteen dogs as ones he had already met today. There were human scents too, a blend of men and women and ranging in ages which he could tell by a variety of factors such as the selection of soap, the drugs they took to combat certain afflictions ... Rex's nose was a wonder to behold.

Nearing the bridal suite, Buster moved across to one side of the corridor so that he was hugging the wall with his body. Or rather, he was attempting to hug the wall but because he's a bulldog all he was doing was rubbing his fur along it at a height of about eighteen inches.

"*What are you doing now?*" sighed Rex.

Buster glanced over one shoulder to find his new sidekick, Cherry Bomb, doing exactly as he was, and the giant German Shepherd was yet again refusing to play along when there was so much fun to be had.

"*Shhhhh, Hell Fang!*" Buster insisted. "*The dognappers might have left guards behind to prevent us from picking up his trail.*"

"Hell Fang?" Rex questioned. *"That's even worse than your previous attempts."* Putting the silly names to one side, Rex pointed out, *"There's no one ahead of us. I would be able to smell them if there were, and besides, the door is open."*

This was news to Buster who hadn't thought to look.

Rex went around his two companions, strolling confidently into the bridal suite, not that he knew that was what it was. All that mattered to him was the whiff of Pomeranian. It had been growing in strength and was undeniably originating from the room he now stood in.

"Oh, yeah, that's a Pomeranian all right." Rex drew in a deep nose full of the scent-laden air and closed his eyes as he committed all of it to memory. There were so many odours to diffuse, but he recognised most of them for what they were and filed each away should he need them for future reference.

Then his eyes snapped open, and his ears folded down as he caught a whiff of something he wished he didn't recognise.

"What is it?" ask Lila, picking up on the larger dog's body language.

"Laxatives," Rex replied with a shudder.

Lila paused to sniff the air for herself, lifting her nose and moving it around as she attempted to find the source of the smell.

"Oh, yes," she remarked when she found it.

In one corner of the room, Buster pawed at a rubbish bin until he knocked it over with a clunk.

"*It's coming from this,*" he sniffed the top of an empty bottle.

Unhappy to be reminded of the episode with the laxatives, Rex elected to leave the room. He had what he'd gone there for and could see no reason to delay moving on. However, just as he got to the door, a light breeze shifted the air in the room, carrying with it a scent that he might otherwise have missed.

Automatically, his top lip curled slightly to expose his teeth.

"*Did you just get that too?*" ask Lila.

Rex growled. "*Evil.*"

Lila joined him. "*And smug self-satisfaction.*"

They looked at each other, and simultaneously spat the word, "*Cat.*"

Buster harrumphed. "*Amber got here first.*"

Lila didn't know who Amber was and was quickly caught up by Buster as the three dogs left the bridal suite, their noses filled with Ernie's scent.

"*She's not going to find Ernie first though, is she?*" Lila thought it was strange that a cat would even bother looking.

Buster exhaled a hard breath before admitting, "*It wouldn't be the first time. She only does it to annoy me, but she caught a whole team of burglars not so long ago. Well, we did, and I want to be clear that the cats could not have succeeded without the dogs, but yeah, there's a chance she might beat us to it.*"

"Not on my watch," snapped Rex, his opinion of cats much the same as every other dog. He'd had his fair share of run-ins with the feline species, and it rarely ended well. The miserable moggies never played fair, that was the problem. The best any dog could hope for was a draw.

About to regale his companions with a story about a gang of scraggly alley cats with whom he had arranged a delicately balanced truce to defeat a mutual enemy, Rex's words were cut off by the sound of a cat squealing loudly. It was followed by a worrying cacophony of furious barks.

Jolted into action, Buster blurted a single word, "*Amber!*" and started running.

How a Cat Does It

A mber had found her way to the bridal suite via a tree not long after taunting Buster and Rex in the garden. It was the bride's dog she was looking for; therefore, to her mind, the bride's room was an obvious place to start.

There were still humans in the room at the time, half a dozen of them, not that Amber could count or had any notion of simple arithmetic beyond knowing that any number greater than zero dogs in her life made for a badly balanced equation.

The people inside hadn't noticed her as she peered in through the open window high above their heads and never once looked her way because, unlike a dog, she had the ability to remain silent. Buster would have given himself away in a heartbeat by panting, scratching at his undercarriage, burping, farting, or otherwise making unnecessary noise.

She remained in the tree for some time, observing the behaviour inside through a window that was open for ventilation and might have stayed there had the humans inside not suddenly all left. Several of them had wandered off during the time she had been watching, but an argument had broken out in the corridor beyond the bridal suite which left the room abandoned.

Climbing in through the window, Amber had proceeded to nose around.

She could smell the dog had been there, but unlike Rex and many of the other dogs staying at the hotel this weekend, she could not then follow the scent. Oh, in theory she could move around and figure out where the dog had gone, which was sort of like tracking the smell by picking up when it was stronger or weaker, but that was what a dog would do and therefore absolutely not a tactic any self-respecting cat would ever consider employing.

No, Amber intended to figure it out by watching the humans.

Emerging from the bride's room, she climbed back down through the tree to find a comfortable spot from which she could observe the gardens. Passing a nest of chittering starling chicks, she gave brief consideration to 'accidentally' knocking it out of the branch it had been woven into.

It would provide a moment's amusement, but seemed like a lot of effort, so she had sauntered past while the tiny, flightless birds eyed her with wonder. She came to a stop where a large bough provided a flat surface.

There, she had begun to wash herself, content that she could multitask without her preening routine affecting her ability to spot a human doing something they ought not to be.

That moment came sooner than she expected.

If there was one advantage to a cat's naturally devious nature, it was that they could spot other creatures acting the same way. With her right front paw hanging in the air where she had been washing it, she squinted at the human hurrying around the side of the hotel.

"Now that's a guilty walk if ever I saw one," Amber murmured to herself. She placed her right paw back on the branch and rose to stand on all four paws. Holding where she was, she continued to watch as the human checked over their shoulder every few steps to see if anyone was following or noticing where they were going.

Amber had to shift position to continue watching when her view of the person was blocked by leaves on the tree and eventually accepted that she was going to have to continue on foot.

It was her focus on the target that got her into trouble.

Too busy watching the human, she didn't check the surrounding area for dogs. Running to keep the person in sight, it was only once she was too far away from the tree that she realised her error.

A Bernese Mountain dog stepped out to block her path.

"Hello, kitty," he grinned as if he'd said something funny.

Amber stopped, quickly scanning her immediate area for something to climb. That she could scale a tree to leave a dog barking brainlessly beneath her was one of the best things about being a cat.

There were no trees, and a sixth sense sent a wave of dread creeping over her fur coat as Amber's hindbrain delivered a simple message: you're in trouble.

The Bernese was far enough away that she could dismiss him momentarily, but spinning around to face a danger she knew was going to be there, Amber found a Doberman staring down at her.

Cerberus grinned, showing his teeth to the fluffy cat because he so desperately wanted her to run. It's no fun if they don't run.

Amber froze. It wasn't just the Doberman; he had a host of other dogs splayed out to his left and right. Deep inside her brain, she knew the right thing to do was to roll on her back with all her claws extended so she could then shred anything that was stupid enough to get within slashing distance. She knew it was the right thing to do, that didn't mean she was brave enough to try it.

And when the Doberman barked, "Boo!", she turned tail and ran.

Sibling Rivalry

On my way down to the hotel bar on the ground floor, my head filled with a variety of scenarios in which my big sister was going out of her way to cause me strife. She had picked on me when we were little and had forever been a thorn in my side. Even when we were adults and living separate lives married to different men in different towns, it had still fallen to me to keep our relationship alive for the sake of our parents' feelings.

Ginny didn't care though. She kept a contemptuous comment loaded in her arsenal at all times and aimed it at me whenever we met. She'd managed to give birth and I hadn't. In my head, that ought to garner sympathetic remarks, not barbs to highlight how I was failing as a woman.

It wasn't the only subject by which she chose to torture me.

It took decades for me to realise how jealous she was of my successful career, the stupid woman never understanding how swiftly I would have swapped it all to be a mother. I have money. So what?

And when her husband finally woke up to how little value, pleasure, or enjoyment his wife brought to his life, the first person she turned to was me. Like a fool I took her in and now she rewarded me by causing problems in my place of work.

By the time I came into the bar, my gauges were in the red and I was ready to blow a gasket. Pausing in the doorway for just long enough to confirm what August had told me, I heard for myself what my sister was saying.

Ginny was holding court and had a glut of the Moscovitch's wedding guests listening to her thoughts on marriage whether they wanted to hear it or not.

"It's all a pointless sham," she preached. "Women signing away their lives ... their vitality, and for what? The ridiculous concept of love? Let me tell you, ladiesh," she slurred. "You might think you are happily married, but can any of you truthfully claim that you never catch your husband looking at another woman? Eh? Eyeing up the derriere of the girl in front of him in the supermarket. She's twenty years younger than you and he's twenty times more successful than he was."

Ginny had a large, yet empty, balloon glass in her right hand that had undoubtedly once contained a silly amount of gin.

I aimed for her, weaving through a bar packed with the guests I was supposed to be hosting. My sister spotted me before I could get to her.

"Look! Here she ish. My little shister. Felishity has an even better shtory to tell than me. Her husband ..." She made a thoughtful face, "whatshisname, he went and died on her." She divulged information no one needed to know. "How about that?" she quizzed her unwilling audience.

A member of the hotel's bar staff encouraged her to put the glass down and speak at a lower volume.

"No!" she snatched the empty glass away, spilling a little melt water and ice onto the floor. "I'm sharing important life facts. Important!" she repeated, looking around the bar to make eye contact with as many patrons as possible. "And you should all lishen and be wary."

I barged my way through the last few feet, making apologies as I went, but never slowing down. Arriving at Ginny's side, I clamped her right forearm in both hands to stop it moving, then used my right hand to pluck the gin glass from it.

"You've had enough," I stated, giving her my unqualified opinion.

"My little shister, everyone," she addressed the crowded bar. "Wedding planner to the stars. And to you lot," she added, unable to stop herself from flinging in another insult.

Snaring her wrist in a vicelike grip, I began to drag her from the bar.

"You are embarrassing me, Ginny, but more than that, you are embarrassing yourself."

She yanked her arm from my grip.

"I'm telling theesh people how it is," she spat back at me. "Better they know now than waste their years on foolish dreams."

I shot out my hand, trying to catch hold of her again, but she danced away and bumped into a man in a summer suit, spilling his pint of beer.

"I'm so sorry," I offered the man and his party my most apologetic face as I chased after Ginny. "Ginny, come on, you have to leave."

"Why?" she shot back. "Why do I have to leave?"

Okay, I'd tried to do it quietly. I'd tried to take her out of the room so we could 'have a little chat', but she wanted to force my hand and right now, right here, I was fine with that.

"Because nobody wants you here." I let the words reverberate. I'd said them loud enough that everyone in the bar heard them and had stopped their own conversations to listen. "No one wants you anywhere, Ginny. Do you know why?" I posed a question I was never going to let her answer. "Because you are a spiteful, hate-filled old cow." I supplied the answer. "Your husband didn't ask for a divorce because he was chasing another woman, but because you utterly neglected him."

Ginny looked like I'd slapped her face.

"What? You weren't expecting the truth from me?" I scoffed. "When did you last pay me a compliment?" I asked her. "When did you last have something nice to say to me? You tortured me when we were children and never let up when we grew to be adults. You got the best of everything being the eldest. I had all the hand-me-downs. And now that you have ruined your marriage, you want to tell these lovely people they have the same thing coming? Well, they don't, Ginny!" I was an unstoppable force now. Or so I thought.

"You were their favourite!" Ginny screamed in my face.

My next words died on my lips.

"No, I wasn't," was all I could think of to say.

A single tear left the corner of Ginny's right eye and rolled down her face.

"Yes, you were," she replied in a quiet voice few in the bar would have been close enough to hear. "You always were from the moment you were born. I was old by then. Too old to be cute and they doted on you because you were the baby."

I had no words that I could find. Was I finally hearing a reason why my big sister had been so cruel to me for so many years? It was all inside her head, but that didn't mean I wasn't hearing the truth about what had motivated her.

"Then you got bigger and pulled all that nonsense about being able to talk to the family pets," Ginny cried. "You craved attention, Felicity. You always have, and you lied, and lied, and lied to make sure my parents could only see you. I was the cuckoo, forced from the nest by the newest baby to arrive."

It wasn't a great time to correct her analogy, so I let the cuckoo thing go.

I also chose to keep quiet about my ability to talk to my pets. As is always the case, no good could possibly come from it.

Ginny was crying and from wanting to throttle her a few moments ago, I had no argument left in me.

I held out my right hand, beckoning with my fingers that she should take it and we should leave the bar.

Accepting her fate without argument, she put her hand in mine and we left the wedding guests behind.

Pack Mentality

Rex easily outpaced the other two dogs as they raced through the hotel to find an exit. He could not be sure if the one they came in through was the nearest or not, but it was the one he knew how to find.

Reaching it, he discovered it was closed and knew from experience that he would not be able to operate the handle to open it.

Coming up fast behind him, Buster yelled, *"I'll get it!"*

Unsure exactly what that meant, Rex had to leap to his left when the bulldog came barrelling directly for him.

Buster, in full Devil Dog mode, and with his new sidekick, Cherry Bomb, egging him on, lowered his skull and with a trumpet of, *"Dun, dun, DAH!"* he rammed the door.

Rex watched it all, too shocked by what he was witnessing to question it or shout a warning.

A resounding thump reverberated through the hotel, but the door chose to ignore Newton's third law and refused to budge even so much as a fraction of an inch.

Buster bounced off, hitting the carpet and rolling onto his back. He came to rest at Rex's feet with the German Shepherd looking down at him.

"I'm not sure whether you are brave or bonkers, but you are definitely dangerous."

"That's right, Beelezedog," Buster tried out a new name which he'd just thought up and felt went nicely with his own superhero name, *"I am dangerous."* He rolled back onto his paws, doing his best to ignore the pain coming from his skull, shoulders, neck, teeth, um, paws, face, eyes ... you get the picture, and joined Lila in barking at the door to be let out.

It was an old dog trick, and one humans had learned to respond to a millennia ago. Heck, even when the first dogs lived in caves with primitive man there had probably been a signal to say, *"Hey, man, I need to go outside, and it is in your best interest to help me in this quest. Otherwise, there's going to be a steaming pile on the cave floor very soon."*

In less than five seconds, a person appeared, diverting their route to see what the ruckus might be about. Unsure what they ought to do, the person elected to open the door the three dogs clearly wished to be on the other side of.

The moment daylight appeared, Rex, Buster, and Lila all smashed their heads through the gap, forcing the door to fly open.

"You're welcome," called the human as they closed it again, but the dogs were long gone.

On the other side of the hotel, scanning the gardens for any sign of his dog, Albert's ears delivered a message.

"That's my dog," he announced abruptly.

Helping with the search, Mike Atwell asked, "How can you be so sure?"

Albert was already walking at speed, heading back toward the hotel's front façade. Twisting at the waist and continuing to walk, he said, "Because it sounds like utter bedlam and that's Rex's specialty."

Utter bedlam described the scene perfectly.

Amber, racing to escape the Doberman, had found herself steered away from the hotel and its sense of sanctuary by the other dogs. Under Cerberus's instructions, they had fanned out to make sure the cat had to head for the trees around the periphery of the garden.

It would need to pick a big one or the dogs might be able to knock it down, but the intention was not to kill the cat, just to have some fun, and maybe beat it up a bit.

Running for her life, all Amber knew was that she wished she'd stayed in Felicity's room. She could have let Buster have this one, but her pride and a desire to annoy the bulldog had driven her from the comfortable sunspot in the window. Now there were dogs all around and they were going to catch her.

Driven ... no, herded, Amber realised, away from the building, the only safe haven she could see were the big oak and sycamore trees at the edge of the garden some fifty yards away. Tearing through a flower bed, she cared not for what damage the pack of dogs on her heels might do; her only thoughts were for survival.

Right on her tail, Cerberus was enjoying the chase. His human insisted on owning a cat and he hated it with deep passion. Cats were always just so snarky and righteous. Well, the one he was forced to tolerate had soon learned her place. It was an old scraggly thing now, with a chunk of ear missing where Cerberus got bored one day and made a point of how much bigger, younger, and more powerful he was.

The cat had avoided him ever since.

Maybe this cat would look good with a chunk of ear missing too.

Coming from the opposite direction, as Amber pelted counterclockwise through the gardens, Rex, Buster, and Lila were heading for the cat at a tangential angle.

Cerberus and his chasing pack spotted the approaching dogs and assumed they were coming to join the fun. It wasn't until they got within a few yards that Cerberus realised something was wrong with their trajectory.

Going slow so he wouldn't leave Buster behind Rex asked, *"Remind me again why we are racing to save the cat. I thought you said you hated her."*

"I do," replied Buster with a shrug. *"She's the most loathsome creature any dog has ever been forced to endure. But she's also my cat and nobody gets to beat her up but me."*

Rex wasn't sure quite how to reply to that. He'd never lived with a cat so had no frame of reference. He wouldn't hurt one, not badly at least, but he was quite ruthless at chasing them out of his garden whenever they ventured beyond the perimeter fence.

With the cat now in sight, Rex could also see how many dogs were giving chase - there were a lot of them.

"You want me to take this one?" he asked

Buster rasped, *"No. He's mine."* It was clear that he meant Cerberus.

Rex could have outpaced the bulldog easily. So too could Lila and while we are at it, a hedgehog with a limp would have given Buster a decent race, but Amber had seen him coming and had arced her route, leaning into the turn until she was running straight for him.

With the animals closing on each other at a tremendous pace, Amber zipped between Rex's legs as he leapt over her, and Buster ploughed directly into Cerberus's chest.

Or he would have done if the Doberman hadn't guessed Buster's attack strategy and nimbly stepped out of the way.

Committed to his battering ram tactic, Buster met with thin air and had to crash into the grass just so he could stop himself and turn around.

Rex stood his ground, giving the cat time to escape. One quick check over his shoulder confirmed she had vanished into the undergrowth and was now too far away for the dogs to catch.

Buster tried to get back to his feet, but Cerberus was already standing over him, his teeth bared as he challenged Buster to start the fight.

"What's the matter, little doggy? Scared are we?"

Buster bared his own teeth.

"Tell your pack to back off and let's see how you do one to one!"

"Ha!" scoffed the Doberman, laughing in Buster's face. *"That's not how packs work."* Switching his focus to glare at Lila, he added, *"You chose poorly with these two losers, doll."*

Lila snarled, *"Doll! You can call me Cherry Bomb!"*

Her bark silenced the other dogs, who all looked at each other, checking to see if anyone understood the reference. Then, as one, they burst out laughing.

Buster rolled onto his paws. If the Doberman was going to attack, then Buster wanted him to get on with it. He wasn't going to listen to Cerberus talk rubbish either way.

"Let me guess," Cerberus managed between guffaws, *"You've got some daft, secret superhero name too."*

Buster growled, *"I am Devil Dog, and the night fears me."*

It brought fresh howls of laughter from the other dogs who were following their alpha's lead, even though some thought a superhero name might be cool to have.

Boldly and confidently, Rex walked through the assembly of dogs. His hackle was not raised, and his face was largely set to neutral. Sure, he was a big dog, but there were other big dogs around. More than anything he was badly outnumbered.

Not that he was scared. Rex was walking with confidence because despite Cerberus's bluster and their superior numbers, Rex doubted the pedigree pooches were actually willing to get into a dustup.

He walked directly past Cerberus as if he were not there and spoke to Buster.

"Come along. We still have a mystery to solve."

Buster had to fight to keep his emotions in check and the intent to snap a comment at the pack alpha was obvious in his expression.

Sensing that his new friend was going to complicate matters, Rex whispered in Buster's ear.

"Leave him be. There are too many of them and Cerberus is not worth the effort."

Buster's top lip twitched as he fought to keep from saying the thoughts in his head. What he wanted to do was put the muscular Doberman on his back in front of his pack, but Rex wasn't wrong, they were at a disadvantage.

Biting down on his pride, Buster nodded his head just once to acknowledge the German Shepherd was right, and with that the two dogs began to walk away again. Cherry Bomb fell in behind them as they made their way through the pack.

"Shouldn't your tails be between your legs, fellas?" jeered Cerberus.

The fresh insult was one too many for Buster. With an explosion of energy, he spun through one hundred and eighty degrees, his lips retracting to expose his teeth as the blood rushed to his head. Thinking time was over and he was going to act on pure instinct.

However, his path to Cerberus was blocked. A Rottweiler, a Great Dane and an Irish Wolfhound had moved into position and were growling down at the bulldog. To get to the alpha, Buster would have to go through all three guards first.

Even with his brain now wired for attack, Buster knew this was not a fight he could win. Between them, Rex and Lila guided him back towards the hotel and the direction in which Amber had gone.

wHaT NexT?

Leaving the hotel bar with my sister, it was clear that Ginny was once again a little the worse for gin. Senselessly drowning the ashes of her marriage, she was caught in a cycle of self-destructive behaviour. Part of me wanted to be sympathetic towards her, yet years of ill behaviour and now her suggestion that I brought it on myself because I claimed an unfair percentage of our parents' available time, were combining to make me think unkind thoughts instead.

She offered no resistance as I towed her out of the bar and most unlike herself, she didn't respond when a few hecklers wished her good riddance.

The wedding was a mess, but with the exception of the missing dog, I believed it was salvageable. The bridesmaids might not look their best in the photographs but as long as they could stand upright and force a smile for a few seconds, the ceremony could go ahead.

What worried me most was that I still didn't have any idea who was behind the sabotage and that meant there could be worse yet still to come.

Vince had promised to look into Primrose's involvement ... well, actually he had bargained to find Ernie with the promise that I would go on ten dates with him. Was I off the hook if he found the dog, but Primrose wasn't behind it? Did I want to be off the hook?

Like Mr Moscovitch, Primrose was up to something. That could not be denied, but my earlier conviction that my rival was behind it all had been eroded. I just didn't see how she could be.

"I need to lie down," Ginny announced quietly, one hand on her forehead. "I think I should have eaten something first."

A spike of horror made me ask, "You're not going to throw up, are you?"

She shook her head, though she chose not to speak.

I thumbed the button to call the elevator and heard someone calling my name before it could arrive. I wanted to get Ginny back to her room before Mindy saw her. Ginny was a disaster, and our relationship was fraught at the best of times, but there was nothing to be gained by letting her daughter see the state she was in.

"Mrs Philips?" Mrs Moscovitch had her hand up to attract my attention as she hurried my way. "Felicity?"

Dealing with Ginny, I'd momentarily forgotten about the maid of honour. It hadn't seemed any more important than the rest of the tasks on my list and Denise's mum was a far better person to deal with such a delicate problem than the wedding planner.

"Is Denise all right?" I asked, wishing the elevator would hurry up. I had so much to do and none of it was getting done. Or maybe it was getting done – Justin, Mindy, and Philippe attending to the necessary tasks, but until I knew we were on track, I wasn't going to be able to relax.

"Well, that's just it, Felicity. I can't find her. You said she was in the lobby restroom?"

"Yes." I frowned my surprise that Mrs Moscovitch hadn't been able to locate her eldest daughter.

"That one over there?" Mrs Moscovitch pointed.

"Really? Denise wasn't in there? Did you call her?"

"And sent a text message," the mother of the bride added.

I didn't feel a need to confirm it hadn't been answered and a solid ball of worry bloomed in my gut. First the bride's dog goes missing, then the food is ruined. While we were reeling from that, the bride's ex-boyfriend turned up with a message that was clearly sent from the bride's phone in an attempt to drive a wedge between the happy couple. We had still been trying to prevent that incident from halting the wedding when Denise fell ill along with the rest of the bridesmaids, a heavy dose of laxatives creating a problem for each of them that no one ought to wish on their worst enemy.

Had someone now done something to Denise? Had she been kidnapped from under our noses?

Mrs Moscovitch was thinking the same thing, her eyes showing the worry she felt.

The elevator pinged, the doors parting to reveal Mr Moscovitch inside. He was hiding something behind his back, his left hand deliberately tucked out of sight. It made my heart thump.

Was he holding a gun? Vince warned me not to let him know I was suspicious and here I was gawping at him with wide eyes.

"Denise?" he rumbled in his accented, deep bass voice.

Mrs Moscovitch wailed, "No! I don't know where she is!"

"I need to lie down," repeated my sister whose arm I still held.

How could I possibly manage to juggle all these problems at the same time? Which thing should I do first? I couldn't call one of my assistants; they were already busy doing all the things I wasn't.

Reversing Ginny, who was looking more and more inebriated by the minute, into a chair set next to a small table and a bookshelf, I said, "Stay here. I'll come back for you."

"But I need to go to bed," Ginny cried. Looking into my eyes, her face crumpled, and she grabbed at my clothing. "Why did he leave me!"

she wailed loud enough that the conversation in the bar paused. "I'm fifty-nine, Felicity! How am I supposed to start again now?"

Oh, dear God.

Had I somehow deserved this? Was the good Lord punishing me for something? I couldn't imagine why, but the question rattling around in my head was, 'What next?'.

"I can take her up to her room," offered Mr Moscovitch, employing the most words in a single sentence since I met him.

Horrified, I snapped, "No!" Then more calmly, "I mean, no thank you, Mr Moscovitch. My sister will be just fine where she is for a few minutes." It was an outright lie. Ginny's head was buried in my dress, undoubtedly leaking tears directly into the fabric along with mascara and goodness knows what else. Regardless, I wasn't going to send her off with the gangland hoodlum.

Of course, I was yet again making a scene in the hotel lobby and August was heading my way.

Getting in first, I said, "We have a missing person!" It was sufficiently shocking to stave off whatever he was about to say, and I followed it with, "It's the maid of honour. Someone poisoned her and the bridesmaids and now the maid of honour is nowhere to be found."

"Oh, my goodness," gasped August, horrified to have so much drama to manage in one day. Flicking his gaze to the bride's parents, he asked, "Your daughter is missing?"

Mr Moscovitch came to his wife's side, slipping something heavy and chunky into his trouser pocket in a move no one was supposed to see. I saw it because I couldn't take my eyes off the arm he had continued to hide and now the bulge in his trousers really did look like a gun.

Mrs Moscovitch snivelled, "Yes, I think she might be."

August looked like he couldn't believe it. He started back toward the reception desk. "I should call the police."

I agreed with him, not that I said the words.

Mrs Moscovitch asked, "What are we going to do, Felicity? Who is behind it all?"

I had no idea.

THE STRENGTH OF TEAMWORK

R ex led Buster and Lila away from the show dogs, all three ignoring the jibes and taunts that followed them.

Rex was not used to allowing anyone the upper hand and it did not sit well. At the same time, he did not wish to let thoughts of revenge cloud his mind. Finding the missing Pomeranian would serve best as a demonstration of his superiority – he would rise above the brainless stupidity of Cerberus and his pack.

Of course, if he got the chance to scent mark the Doberman's head from a balcony then he absolutely would.

The cat was no longer in the bushes, not that he'd expected it to stay put, but its scent was easy to follow. Buster and Lila could follow it too, all three dogs angling back toward the hotel on a winding path through the gardens.

Getting close to the source of the scent, Rex looked for the cat, and caught movement from the corner of his eye.

"*Hey,*" called Amber, eight feet off the ground in a silver birch tree. "*Can I come down?*"

Buster answered, "*Sure. Why not?*"

Amber moved one paw, but otherwise showed little sign she felt it was safe to descend.

"*The other dogs,*" she remarked. "*Are they going to chase me? I've had my fill of being chased today.*"

She was referring of course to Rex and Lila, two dogs she didn't know. She doubted it helped that she'd met the German Shepherd earlier and was rude to him. Well, she called it rude now, but really she was just being a cat. What else was she supposed to do?

"*We just rescued you from Cerberus and his pack,*" Lila pointed out. "*We didn't do it so we could chase you ourselves.*"

Buster stared up into the tree. "*You can come down, Amber. None of us will chase you, but you have to promise to keep your snarky comments to yourself.*" When Amber appeared to be debating his demand, he added, "*I mean it, Amber. If you start getting all ... catty with us, the deal is off.*"

"*Ok, ok,*" she didn't like it, but the scruffy, smelly bulldog *had* come to her aid when she needed him.

Climbing down out of the tree, she sucked in her pride and went over to him, rubbing against his chest and shoulder affectionately.

Buster, being stared at by Rex and Lila, coughed loudly, "*Yes, well, like I said to Rex earlier. If anyone is ever going to bite you, they need to get behind me in the queue.*"

Rex rolled his eyes. The cat and dog lived together and though they clearly got on each other's nerves and wound the other up continually, there was also great affection between them.

"*Come on,*" Rex started walking again. "*That missing dog isn't going to find himself. We need to go back to the bridal suite to see if we can pick up Ernie's scent. It will be hard to follow otherwise.*"

"*Ah,*" said Buster. "*That's a problem.*"

Lila cocked one eyebrow. "*Why?*"

"*The scent vanishes just outside the door,*" explained Buster. "*My bet is that he was carried. He might even have been inside a bag or a box.*"

Rex blinked. "*You didn't think to share this with us earlier?*"

None of the dogs noticed, but Amber was smiling smugly to herself.

Buster tried not to sound too defensive when he pointed out, "*You wanted to capture Ernie's smell. At no point did you highlight a desire to track it from the source.*"

"*How else was I supposed to do it?*" Rex questioned. "*If we can't track it, and you think he was either carried or stuffed inside a box, the only way we are going to find him is by accident.*"

Lila chipped in, "*Whoever carried him will have picked him up. Ernie's scent will be on their clothes. If we can find a human with his scent, then we have our suspect, surely.*"

"*That's good in theory,*" lamented Rex, "*but he was in the bridal suite. How many humans did you smell in there?*"

Buster huffed, "*A dozen or more.*"

Amber realised how much she was smiling and straightened her face before Buster saw. Having just promised to not be superior (even though she was), and snarky (even though that was her baseline start point for addressing any dog), she figured she should be helpful instead.

"*I believe I might have a solution,*" she volunteered. She had to stop at that point because offering to help the dogs without a tangible gain on her part was leaving her feeling a little woozy and the alien words had left her mouth feeling a little strange.

The dogs had stopped talking to hear what Amber had to offer, so when she saw them waiting expectantly, she forced herself to continue.

"*I saw a human moving suspiciously.*"

"*Suspicious how?*" Rex wanted to know. He was adept at picking out the guilty human in a group.

Amber recalled what she had seen. "*The person was hurrying and checking over their shoulders to make sure no one was watching or following. Now I cannot say for certain that is the same person who took the little dog; they didn't have anything in their hands …*"

"*Wait, wait, wait,*" Rex interrupted, now in full police dog mode. "*Are we talking about a male human or a female human?*"

Amber thought about the question. Unlike the dogs, she couldn't do it on smell, and so far up in the tree, she wouldn't have been able to smell the person anyway. Casting her mind back to what the human looked like – not something a cat would usually notice – she was able to recall certain features.

"*A female,*" she stated confidently. "*I think,*" she added a moment later. With all three dogs frowning at her, she grumpily pointed out, "*I was in a tree, okay? The person had long hair, that means it was a woman, right?*"

Rex sucked some air between his teeth. "*Most of the time, but the hair thing is not exclusive to one or the other.*"

Amber frowned and racked her brain. "*The person had a bag on their arm. Felicity always carries a bag.*"

Rex shrugged. "*Same answer. Male humans carry a bag sometimes. I suppose there's no point asking you about smell?*"

Amber growled, "*I was in a tree. Look, their movements had devious written all over them, and I was following him or her when Cerberus cornered me. That was just a few minutes ago and I saw where the 'person' was heading.*"

That was good enough for Buster. "*Come on then, Amber. Let's see if we get lucky.*"

STALLING FOR TIME

Albert puffed his way past the front of the hotel, scanning in every direction for any sign of his dog. Given how much noise he'd heard from the other side of the building, there had to be a large number of dogs involved.

He also thought he'd heard a cat, but rounding the side of the hotel and wishing he was fifty years younger ... heck, twenty years would do, Albert slowed to a walk.

There were dogs everywhere again. The bigger ones were easy to pick out – Irish Wolfhound, Great Dane, Labrador Retriever – and he could see lots of smaller ones too – spaniels, terriers, a miniature poodle, but of his own dog there was no sign.

"See him anywhere?" asked Mike Atwell, staring at the hotel gardens too.

Humans were gathering the dogs. Whatever had transpired was over and had caused enough noise that the owners were racing to retrieve their prized pedigree.

Albert watched as several people inspected their dogs, chastising them vocally for getting up to no good.

A large Doberman with a proud physique was leading the procession back toward the hotel, the man attached to him looked like a groom in full morning suit and top hat.

Albert puffed out his cheeks and muttered under his breath. He could have answered Mike, but chose to employ his voice for a different task. That of bellowing his dog's name.

"REX!" he waited to see if he got any kind of reaction, though his dog wasn't known for answering. "REX!"

Mike joined in, his hands cupped around his mouth to channel his shout, "REX!"

Albert was going to shout again, but something had caught his eye. Tracking it through the distant trees where they bordered the edge of the property, there was no mistaking the reflective blue and yellow stripes running down the side of not one but three police cars.

Turning ninety degrees to face Mike, he gave a sorry shake of his head.

"You were just stalling," he levelled an accusation at the detective sergeant. "Why couldn't you have just said that instead of pretending to help me?"

Mike's eyebrows met in the middle as he tried to figure out what the older man was saying.

"I'm not following. Stalling for what?"

Albert thrust out his right arm, arrowing it at the bonnet of the lead car which had just turned down the long driveway toward the hotel.

"Is that Quinn?" Albert snapped. "You could have had him back here hours ago when you first spotted me. Has this all been about getting the most information out of me? Think this will be a good collar, do you?" Albert was feeling betrayed and angry. "An old man who couldn't have escaped you even if he wanted to." Never in his life had he ever had sympathy for any innocent suspect who chose to lash out at their arresting officer, yet right now he was giving serious consideration to kicking Mike Atwell in the shin.

Mike followed Albert's arm, his own heart sinking when he saw the police cars. They were driving at a sedate pace, not blasting along the road as if on their way to stop a major crime. There were three of them though, and not only did that almost certainly mean Chief Inspector Quinn, who loved to travel with an entourage, but it also meant they were responding to a serious crime.

Two seconds ago, Mike's path had been clear to him. He was going to help the old man to leave the area and was putting some thought into travelling with him to Cornwall. Now Chief Inspector Quinn was bearing down on them, and it had to be because someone had spotted Albert and called the police.

Mike felt his stomach tighten. He'd had plenty of opportunity to arrest Albert and no excuse in the world was going to change what happened when Quinn found out he hadn't. Aiding and abetting, that is what Quinn would call it, and he had the ear of the chief constable.

Grimacing as he chose to face the problem head on, Mike said, "It wasn't me. My guess would be that someone else recognised you and made the call. Either way, there's no point running now."

Albert heard Mike's words and was about to sling them back at him when he decided he was hearing the truth. DS Atwell hadn't been playing him and that meant the man was in just as much trouble as Albert. Probably more, in fact, because Albert was going to be found innocent soon enough. He was wanted for questioning in connection with the explosion in Whitstable, but he hadn't actually done any-thing criminal. Well, not that anyone could tie him to.

Mike, on the other hand, had chosen to disobey an order. Opting to not arrest Albert as he should was in direct violation of his instructions and would land him in hot water.

"Perhaps you should make yourself scarce," Albert suggested. "There's nothing to be gained by getting caught helping me."

Mike shook his head. "No. Let's continue trying to find Rex. They won't know exactly where you are, so we have a few minutes. If you can find him in that time, I can make sure he is taken to someone who will look after him until you are released. The last thing you want is him going with animal control."

Albert agreed with every word Mike said, and the two hurried on. Past the pedigree dogs being led inside the hotel by their owners, and onward through the gardens.

What neither man could know was that Chief Inspector Quinn had no idea Albert Smith was within spitting distance of his current location. Drawn back to Champney's Resort and Spa Hotel for a second time in just a few hours, he fervently hoped there either really was a missing person this time – a grisly murder would be nice, he needed something juicy to get his name back into the limelight – or that Felicity Philips was behind what would prove to be a crank call and he would be able to prove it this time.

IS THIS WEDDING ON OR OFF?

"**M**rs Philips," sneered the chief inspector as he entered the hotel lobby and immediately clapped his eyes on me.

I'd been fortunate enough that Justin had appeared. The team of wait staff had formed up and he was taking them out to the marquee. There he would make sure they all knew their roles and could perform them to the standard I expected.

He then returned to escort Ginny up to her room. Drunk and vulnerable, my sister chose to embarrass me further by flirting openly with my master of ceremonies. Justin took it in his stride, politely declining her offer of a massage. That was the last thing I heard before the elevator doors closed on them.

Mrs Moscovitch had continued to call Denise while fretting for where she might be and what terrible fate might next befall the wedding. She hypothesised about who could be behind it all, flinging family names at her husband who grunted at each one or sometimes just shrugged. I'd never met a man who spoke so little. He really was the 'strong silent type'.

What surprised me most, given what I knew about Mr Moscovitch, was that his wife never once lowered her voice to ask if the problems could be due to his criminal operations. I desperately wanted to ask Mr Moscovitch if the problems witnessed today could be at the hands of one of his rivals, but to do so would be tantamount to accusing him of criminal behaviour. I wasn't crazy enough for that.

August alerted the hotel staff to be on the lookout and quizzed those working reception about whether they had seen anyone with Denise, seen Denise, or perhaps spotted a person carrying an unconscious form right by their noses.

Obviously, they hadn't, so with Denise's parents fretting over her disappearance, I felt I had to stay by their side.

Now the police were here, and I could not stop myself from watching Mr Moscovitch's face to see how he would react. Just like Vince said, the gang boss was a cool customer, never so much as twitching in the presence of so many uniforms.

Chief Inspector Quinn addressed me when he was still halfway across the lobby, raising his voice and making my name sound like an accusation.

"Chief Inspector," I replied, keeping any negative inflection from my voice. "So good of you to come in person again. I'm sure Mr and Mrs Moscovitch appreciate having a senior officer attend the scene." Whatever I felt about the man, there was a person missing and that was all that mattered.

I stepped to one side, my involvement in what was to follow unnecessary save to confirm that I had seen Denise go into the restroom and had spoken to her when she was in there.

Leaving the bride's parents to speak to the police, I made my excuses and left the hotel lobby.

It's not often that I wish I had a hip flask in my handbag, and it was a good thing I never carried one because today had been trying enough to drive a nun to drink. It wasn't over yet either.

I took the stairs to get back to the first floor, expecting to find them silent. Pausing at the halfway landing, I placed my forehead against the cool wall and closed my eyes.

The day would end and in no time at all I would be soaking in my bath, listening to tranquil music, and basking in the knowledge that I was going to be the one to plan and manage the next royal wedding.

How's that for positive thinking?

The drama of this day, the saboteur, and Mr Moscovitch's scary behaviour would all fade into the past like so much water under the bridge.

Of course, the likelihood of the ceremony going ahead, now that the bride's sister was missing, had reduced to something close to zero. The question of where she was and who might have taken her bounced around in my head as I pushed off the wall and started up the stairs again.

Taking my phone from my handbag, I scrolled to find Justin's number and called him for an update.

"Felicity, I was just about to call you." He walked me through the update I wanted before I even had to ask. "Chef O'Malley is a little more uppity than usual, but everything is on track in the kitchen. The florists have already departed – their work is done, the pastor is here to conduct the ceremony; I think you'll find him in the bar imbibing a glass of sherry and conversing with the wedding guests. The string quartet and harpist are all set up. I could go through the full list if you want, but the short version is that there is nothing much left to do. Incredibly, everything has gone to plan for once. Mindy and Philippe have been of enormous help; that niece of yours is proving to be a real asset."

It was pleasing to hear, and I would talk to her about it later. In the meantime, I asked, "What about Philippe?"

Justin took a second to consider his answer before saying, "I'm not going to say anything negative about him, because of course he's still learning the ropes. He's only been with us a few weeks."

"Buuuuut ..." I encouraged Justin to spit out what he wasn't saying.

"Well, I can't find him, and he seemed quite distracted for the last couple of hours. Constantly on his phone to someone sending messages back and forth. I had to ask him to put it away three times."

I filed the information away. It was something I would deal with on Monday in the office and felt sure it would require only a short conversation about protocol.

Everything was in place, and that was great news, but it still didn't mean the wedding was going ahead. I had reached the top of the stairs and was coming through the door to access the first floor when I started on a list of all the things I wanted Justin to recheck.

Heading along the corridor towards the bridal suite, I argued, "I still think there's a saboteur and the likelihood of them striking again feels very high." With my next stride I turned the corner to come into the corridor leading to the bridal suite and the bride's sister was standing right in front of me.

"Denise!"

Justin's surprised voice filled my ear, "Denise?"

Hurriedly, I ended my call to him. "I've got to go. I'll call you back." Abruptly, and a little rudely, I stabbed the red button to end the call and stuff my phone back into my handbag with hands that couldn't move fast enough. "Denise," I called out as I hurried towards her. She was already looking my way of course, her attention drawn when I first blurted her name. "Where have you been?" I asked. "Everyone's looking for you. The police are here."

"The police? Why would the police be here?" She was standing outside the door to the bridal suite, her face etched with surprise and a little bewilderment.

"Because you went missing," I explained though I thought it ought to be obvious. "I left you in the ladies' restroom and when we came back there was no sign of you. People have been calling you and sending you text messages. You didn't reply to any of them."

"I went for a walk outside," Denise's features were pinched, questioning why it was that she ought to have to defend her actions. "I needed some fresh air, and I didn't have my phone with me." She made a show of looking down at her dress to draw my attention to it. "This thing doesn't come with pockets, and I didn't see a need to take my phone with me while I was dealing with Angus. Plus, I'll be carrying flowers for the ceremony and everyone I might want to speak to is here today."

She said all this while stomping back through to the bridal suite to find her handbag. Snatching her phone from it, her eyes bugged out when she saw the number of missed calls and messages.

"I'd better call mum," she muttered, thumbing the call button, and pressing the phone to her ear.

My heart was still coming back to a more normal pace - seeing Denise in the corridor had made it skyrocket again. The maid of honour wasn't missing at all; she never was. Chief Inspector Quinn had been called to the hotel for the second false alarm today. He wasn't going to be pleased about that and I was rather glad none of it was my fault.

I could hear Mrs Moscovitch bawling down the phone. Overcome with relief now that she knew there had never been anything to worry about, the bride's parents were on their way back up to where I was standing.

This wedding was on!

My jubilation was short lived though, for the spectre of a saboteur still hung over my head.

I could hear Donna in the bedroom of the bridal suite. She was getting ready at last. Her dress, the near priceless, and now infamous, Kipling original hung inside a plastic sheath from a hook next to the bedroom door. Getting her into it and making sure everything was as it should be was a task for her bridesmaids. Were they up to it?

I left Denise and the bridal suite to check on Christy, Ellie, and Juniper. They were just around the next corner and that gave me enough time to call Vince.

"Darling." I don't know if it's me or not, but when Vince talks to me it always sounds as if he is deliberately employing a bedroom voice. There is an undertone to it that suggests the words coming from his mouth should make my knickers fall off. "I assume you are calling for an update?"

"Have you found Ernie?" I got straight to the point.

"No, dear. However, I did find the gun Mr Moscovitch was keeping in his bag of golf clubs."

"Oh, my God!" I gasped. I guess it pleased me to learn that I hadn't imagined the whole thing, but at the same time, Mr Moscovitch had a gun with him!

"Don't worry, darling. I've disabled it."

"Disabled?"

"Yes, dear. It's a simple matter of taking out the firing pin and will be quite undetectable until he attempts to use it. No matter what he does now, it will not fire. So if he has got something planned ... well, let's just say no one is going to get hurt."

This had to be one of the craziest weddings I had ever been involved in. I was going to have to start performing background checks on my clients when I wasn't already certain who they were and where their money came from. I was still terrified for what the father of the bride might have planned and was praying that the weapon was precautionary only.

Nearing the bridesmaids' rooms, a fresh thought occurred to me, "Where was the gun? Where had he put the bag of golf clubs?"

Vince chuckled, "It was behind his chair at the top table."

I stopped outside Ellie's door, wanting to finish my conversation with Vince before I went in to check on her. What on earth did Mr Moscovitch have planned for the wedding breakfast? Was this going to be something to do with his speech.

Vince was still chuckling, forcing me to ask, "What is it that you find so amusing about this situation, Mr Slater?"

"Nothing, dear. Nothing at all. I'm watching some dogs out of the window; they are most amusing. I've got to go. I'll catch up with you shortly."

Whatever it was that he was looking at had to be utterly hilarious because he was barely able to get his final words out before he descended into uncontrollable laughter just before the line went dead.

Frowning hard and then worrying that it was going to leave me with even more wrinkles than I already had, I stuffed the phone back into my handbag and knocked on Ellie's door.

cats are superior

Amber, Buster, Lila, and Rex were all staring at a door. The three dogs were in agreement that there was only one human scent leading up to it - one single person had come this way recently.

"*More than once,*" Rex pointed out. "*You can tell by the shoe prints,*" he drew everyone's attention to the marks in the dirt.

"*A female for certain,*" Buster sniffed again and squinted his eyes, then announced, "*I know this scent.*"

Amber failed to hide her surprise, "*Really? You can do that?*" Realising what she had done, she then began licking a paw in a disinterested manner. "*I mean, how interesting. I suppose you're going to tell us you've solved the whole case now.*"

Buster cocked an eyebrow at her. "*I know the scent,*" he explained to Rex and Lila, "*but I couldn't for certain say who it is. I will need to smell them again.*"

"*We all have the scent now,*" Lila pointed out.

The dogs were wagging their tails, excited to have moved their investigation onward, even if only a little bit.

Still licking her paw, Amber asked, "*Can any of you smell the dog?*"

The question was like a slap to the face to the three canines. None of them could smell the missing Pomeranian, so all they had was the track of a female human going to a door in the side of the hotel.

"*Hold on,*" Lila turned her attention on the cat. "*You're the one who led us in this direction.*"

Amber continued licking at her paw and wiping her ear. "*I said I saw someone suspicious. And I did. I never said they had a dog with them.*"

Buster was about to bark his loudest right into Amber's ear. She hated it when he did that which only made him want to do it all the more. They might have called a truce, but she was back to being her usual catty self.

Before he could, Rex interrupted him, "*I think I just heard something.*"

All three dogs strained their hearing, and even Amber stopped pretending to preen herself so she could listen too.

Several beats of silence followed, the four animals stilling their breathing as they employed one of their weakest senses.

Just before Amber could deliver a snarky comment, the tiny sound of a small dog whimpering reached their ears.

"*We've found him!*" barked Rex excitedly, his tail wagging ten to the dozen.

Lila stared up at the barrier blocking their path. "*But he's behind that door.*"

"*We just need a human,*" Buster spun around to look for one and was about to bark when Lila stopped him.

"*It was a human who put Ernie in there. We cannot know who's in on this. We need to rescue him ourselves.*"

Rex agreed entirely. Bouncing up onto his back paws, he placed his front legs against the door to see if it might budge.

"*I think it opens outwards,*" he remarked, pushing off to come back to the ground.

Buster twisted his head all the way to the left and then twisted it all the way to the right. He followed that with a complicated rolling of his shoulders and wiggling of his hips as he limbered up.

Trotting away from the building to get a decent run up, he rasped in his Devil Dog voice, "*Stand back everyone. It's superhero time.*"

Amber smiled, *"Oh, goody. The dog's going to attempt to kill himself again."*

Rex stepped into Buster's path before the bulldog could set off.

"You can't break down the door, Buster."

Lila whispered, *"He's in Devil Dog mode. You need to call him Devil Dog."*

Rex rolled his eyes. *"Whatever. You can't break down the door. You'll just break your skull."*

Amber argued, *"No, he can do it. Let him have a few attempts at least."*

Looking about for an alternative entry point, Rex said, *"There's bound to be another way in. We might have to go through the hotel's main entrance and find our way around."*

Lila joined in. *"This is the back of the hotel. We're just around the corner from the kitchens."* she didn't need to point that out, all three dogs could smell the food being prepared though they were trying hard not to focus on it. *"It might be this is a storeroom."*

The dogs stared at the door again. Above their heads was a sign which none of them could read.

Racking their brains to come up with a new plan, the breeze blowing through the hotel grounds shifted slightly and in doing so created an eddy of air close to where the animals were standing.

Rex's nose caught it first, but the other two dogs were only a half second behind him and they all knew what it meant. They had just caught a proper whiff of Ernie's scent and that meant air had to be getting in and out.

"*There's a way in,*" Rex remarked as he set off to find it.

Buster and Lila fanned out, the three dogs pushing into the undergrowth on either side of the closed door.

"*It's here!*" barked Lila less than two seconds later, her tail sticking out from a clump of weeds.

Within moments, the weeds were flattened by the larger dogs, and they could see a hole where a brick had come loose next to a ventilation plate.

They were sniffing at it, confirming what they already knew. Whatever the room on the other side was, it contained the missing Pomeranian dog.

They had found him.

"*Can you fit through?*" asked Rex, sounding doubtful.

Lila pulled a face but attempted to squeeze her skull into the gap, nevertheless.

Standing back again, she said, "*Not a chance. I can get my head into it, but my shoulders will never fit through. We need someone slimmer than me.*"

The dogs slowly rotated around to stare at the cat.

Feeling the canine eyes upon her, Amber paused mid-lick, her left front paw hanging in the air for a moment.

"*What?*" she asked. It took a heartbeat to realise what they were suggesting and less time than that to begin arguing. "*Uh-uh, no chance pooches. Look at me,*" she demanded. "*I'm a pedigree cat. I do not go into dark places filled with cobwebs. I certainly don't squeeze through narrow spaces where I might get dirt on my beautiful cream coat. Do you slobbering mutts not realise how much effort it takes to look this perfect?*"

In a gentle voice, Buster said, "*You're the only one who can fit, Amber.*"

Amber put her hanging left paw down on the ground and squinted her eyes at him.

"*That's hardly a good reason.*"

Rex matched the timbre of Buster's voice when he pointed out, "*You can be a hero.*"

Amber scoffed at him. "*A hero? I'm a cat. I don't care about being a hero. I'm already a god.*"

Quietly, so only the other two dogs would hear, Lila said, "*I bet we can just stuff her through.*"

Walking over to where the cat sat, Buster employed his most earnest expression.

Misinterpreting it, Amber inquired, "*Do you need to go for a poo?*"

Buster blinked and gave his head a shake to clear it. *"No, Amber. I need you to do the thing the dogs cannot. I need you to demonstrate what you're always saying: that cats are superior to dogs. I know you don't want to get dirty, and you don't know what's on the other side of the wall, but none of the dogs can do this. It's a task only a cat can complete."*

Amber grimaced. She knew she was going to have to do it, however, in accepting her fate, she recognised some opportunity. If Felicity had been asking her, she would have demanded a freshly poached mackerel. Buster could not provide one of those, but there were other advantages she could leverage.

"You will avoid sleeping on the sofa for the rest of the year."

Buster frowned. *"What?"*

"Don't interrupt, Buster, I'm not finished. These are my terms. Take them or leave them."

Buster exhaled a tired sigh. The cat was always moaning about having to share her favourite spots with him. *"No sleeping on the sofa. What else?"*

"No farting in the same room as me. For as long as you live."

Buster looked across at the other dogs to gauge their opinion before answering, *"I'm not sure I can achieve that. Sometimes they sneak up on me when I'm asleep."*

"Then you'll have to do your best, won't you?" replied Amber rather snippily. *"No drinking out of my water bowl. No clearing up what's in*

my bowl when I haven't finished all the food in it. No shaking yourself anywhere near me. You always get slobber on my fur."

"Okay, okay, Amber. I agree to all your terms. Can we get on with rescuing the little dog now?"

Amber's list was getting longer as more and more items occurred to her. Living with the dog was only bearable because she got to torture him on an almost daily basis. The fact that he constantly retaliated only because she was so mean to him had never once entered her head.

"Seriously," remarked Rex. *"Can we get on with this?"*

Firing dagger eyes in the German Shepherd's direction, Amber sauntered nonchalantly across to the hole.

Peering inside, she said, *"I cannot tell what's in there."*

Muttering under her breath, Lila commented, *"I hope it's a T Rex."*

Amber heard what the dachshund said and chose to ignore her. It wouldn't do for a cat to stoop to a dog's level.

Without further comment, she stretched out with her front paws, and wiggled through the tight hole.

GO TIME

With a final check of my watch, I announced that it was time.

"Fifteen minutes, everyone. Please, I need to get everyone except the bride, the bridesmaids and maid of honour, and the father of the bride to make their way down to the marquee now."

The bridesmaids and maid of honour were on their feet and though they looked a little pale and had lost the bubbliness and excitement displayed prior to the incident with the laxatives, they were being real troopers.

Whatever drug the doctor had administered was doing what it was supposed to do: counteracting the effects of the laxative. I doubted any of them were going to want to eat or drink much this evening, but that didn't matter too much so long as Donna and Damien were able to get married.

Justin and Mindy were feverishly running around between all the various elements of the wedding ceremony and the breakfast that was to follow, making sure that no one had messed with anything.

Philippe still hadn't reappeared, but had answered a text message to confirm that nothing untoward had become of him. He didn't answer my follow up message, and we were going to have a serious discussion about that later. However, my focus was very much on the ceremony now. I was going to get Donna and Damien married and nothing was going to stop me.

However, as Mrs Moscovitch, together with a few aunts and residual family members and friends were ushered away, I heard Denise asking, "Are you sure about this, Sis? Are you sure you want to go through with it without Ernie here?"

We had all been steadfastly avoiding the subject of the missing Pomeranian for more than an hour now. Why on earth was the bride's older sister bringing it up minutes before Donna was due to walk down the aisle.

The bride's face crumpled, her misery and worry returning in an instant.

I flared my eyes at the maid of honour, shooting a warning in her direction.

"What?" Denise fired back indignantly. "None of you appreciate what that little dog means to my sister."

"Yes," I growled, "but we're not supposed to be talking about it."

Donna sucked in a shuddering breath and accepted a tissue when Ellie held out a box of them.

Dabbing at an eye, she managed to say, "it's okay, Felicity. I am getting married no matter what. Maybe whoever is behind this will release Ernie when they see that they couldn't stop the wedding. I'm telling myself that he's fine. He's just a pawn in someone else's sick game."

"Exactly that, Donna," agreed Juniper, supporting her friend. The other bridesmaids came around her, the three friends all linking arms to surround Donna in a group hug that left Denise completely side-lined.

I checked my watch again: ten minutes to go. Was there anything to worry about? The question was bouncing around my head like it was stuck inside a pinball machine.

Usually, by this point in the day, I am sipping a gin and tonic and watching from afar, content that everything I could do has already been done and that the baton has been passed to Justin, my master of ceremonies, to run the event itself.

There was no rush to get downstairs - it's fine for the bride to be at least a little bit late, however it genuinely felt like the longer I left it the more likely it was that something would happen, so with that in mind I encouraged Mr Moscovitch and all the ladies to make their way to the elevator.

Nothing happened. The elevator car didn't suddenly stall halfway down as my overactive imagination assured me it might. The lights didn't suddenly go out. The ground didn't split in two beneath our feet, and we walked all the way to the marquee where I could hear the string quartet entertaining the congregation inside.

We paused outside as a group, allowing Mr Moscovitch to position himself next to his daughter. Donna's dress did not possess a train that needed carrying, but the three girls, followed by Denise at the rear, assembled behind the bride.

Peeking through a gap in the canvas door, I nodded to Justin and a few moments later the string quartet wound up the tune they were playing, paused and then began playing the Wedding March.

If something was going to happen to stop the ceremony, it was going to happen any second now.

BICYCLES AND BUTTERFLIES

B uster put his face up next to the hole. "*What can you see?*"

Amber had wriggled through the hole, the tip of her tail vanishing into the darkness just a few seconds before Buster felt the need to ask what she had found.

She didn't answer though.

On the other side of the wall, Amber had dropped nimbly down onto a cardboard box and from there she was allowing her eyes to adjust to the darkness. There was a dog in the room with her; she could smell it and hear it breathing.

"*Ernie?*" she chose to enquire, though she was certain it had to be the right dog - she might loathe Buster, but she couldn't deny that his nose worked rather well.

"*Wassat?*" came a surprised voice. "*He he!*"

Amber's eyebrows took a hike up her forehead at the unexpected response.

"*Ernie?*" she tried again. "*I'm looking for a missing Pomeranian dog. Don't ask me why; it's a long and complicated story. Suffice to say that I stand to gain from your recovery. Now where are you?*"

The voice echoed back from the darkness, "*Bicycles! I hate bicycles!*"

Blinking in the darkness, Amber was able to pinpoint where the voice was coming from but could not see the dog. Nevertheless, she asked, "*How is that germaine to the matter in hand?*"

"*Wheels,*" growled the voice in the darkness. "*That's the problem. Wheels can't be trusted.*"

Despairing, Amber peered over the side of the box, spotted her landing, and jumped down to the ground.

"*Uuurgh!*" she complained, finding the floor to be coated in a damp grimy dust. "*This is going to take ages to get out of my fur.*"

Now that she was at floor level, she understood why she hadn't been able to spot the dog previously - he was tucked beneath a shelf and backed against the wall. Only the dim reflection from his eyes gave him away.

"*Amber!*" Buster barked through the hole above her head again. "*What's taking so long? Have you found him or not? Is he okay?*"

"*Okay?*" she repeated the word to herself. "*That's highly debatable.*"

Walking as delicately as she could, she crossed the floor on her tip toes to keep the long hair on her legs from becoming matted with grime. At the shelf, she muttered several expletives before crouching down to look under it.

Now that she was closer, she could see the small dog easily enough. It was a Pomeranian. A particularly small one less than half her size.

"*Would you like to come out?*" she asked.

"*Can't,*" said Ernie.

Humouring him, Amber asked, "*And why is that? I rather think you'd prefer it if you came with me. There are some dogs who will escort you back to your human. I dare say there will probably be some treats and perhaps even some affection.*" Under her breath she made several comments about the strange behaviour humans demonstrated in tolerating dogs in the first place.

Ernie whimpered in a scared way, "*I haven't got any legs. I can't move.*"

Amber's face formed a confused frown as she counted the three paws that she could see. Then she moved slightly to the right to confirm that the fourth one was also there.

"*I can see your legs, Ernie. They are all there.*"

"No, they're not," he argued. *"The butterfly stole them."*

Amber's mouth opened as a question formed, yet she closed it again without ever voicing the words in her head.

"Do you remember the human who put you in here?"

"Yes," Ernie replied obediently.

"Did they give you something to eat?"

The sound of Ernie's little tail wagging in the dust preceded his excited reply, *"Yes! It was a piece of cheese. There was something crunchy in it."*

Amber sighed again. The dog was stoned. She remembered Buster coming home from a visit to the vets after he'd gotten himself caught in some barbed wire. He needed stitches to a back leg and when he returned, the drugs they had given him were yet to wear off. Buster had been highly open to suggestion which made it one of the best evenings of Amber's life.

Of course, Felicity had arrived home in time to prevent Buster skateboarding down the stairs, but it had been fun up until that point.

Leaving the Pomeranian where he was, Amber jumped back up onto the box and went back to the hole. Buster's face was pressed up against it, his left eyeball looking giant as it peered through from outside.

Because she is a cat and for no other reason, Amber reached out with a paw and batted his face.

"You are blocking out the light, Buster." With Buster rubbing at his eye with one paw, Amber explained the predicament. *"I'm not saying I can't get him out from under the shelf, but there's no chance I'll get him up to this hole to push him out. You're going to have to get help."*

Cat Rescue

Finding themselves all the way around at the back of the hotel, Detective Sergeant Mike Atwell and wanted fugitive of the law, Albert Smith, were beginning to feel that they were never going to find Albert's dog when a cacophony of loud barking filled the air.

It was coming from a spot no more than twenty or so yards from their current position. They could not see the dogs, but Albert recognised Rex's bark when he heard it.

He quickened his pace, bellowing, "Rex!" as loud as he possibly could.

Able to go faster than the retired detective, Mike shot ahead, aiming for a clump of trees. He got there first, finding a gap through the undergrowth that had clearly been walked by someone else recently.

A female someone else, he instantly assessed from the shoe prints left behind in the dirt. There was no time to examine it any further though, because right in front of him were three dogs. They had seen him and were coming his way.

Or so he thought.

The large German Shepherd ignored him completely, brushing by Mike's left thigh as he went in search of his human.

That left a bulldog and a miniature dachshund who ran at his legs, jumped up excitedly while barking madly, and then ran back to a door in the side of the building. They repeated this, making it very clear that they wanted him to open the door for them.

Five yards behind Mike, Albert was being reunited with his dog. Down on one knee, he had an arm wrapped around Rex's neck as he patted and stroked the happy dog.

"Where have you been today, you daft creature?" Albert asked, wishing he could get an answer.

"*I've been solving a crime,*" replied Rex, disappointed that his human couldn't understand him. "*Actually, even though you don't add much value to my investigations, it is more fun solving them when you're around.*" He delivered a lick to Albert's chin, managing to get the tip of his tongue up the old man's left nostril at the same time.

Albert flailed his arms, trying to hug his dog without getting his teeth cleaned at the same time.

"Get off me, you slobbering mutt," Albert laughed, using Rex as an anchor to pull himself back to upright. Mike had disappeared into the bushes and the other dogs Albert had heard barking were now silent. "Have you found something, Mike?"

Mike was looking at the door. The sign on the outside of it read 'Pump Room' and the warning symbol beneath it suggested there were corrosive chemicals stored or used within.

The Detective Sergeant expected to find that this was something to do with the hotel's swimming pool, but whatever it was, the two dogs at his feet seemed very determined to get inside.

"What is it?" he asked them. "What's inside here that's got you so excited?"

Buster barked a reply, "*Ernie the missing Pomeranian is inside there. So is my human's cat for that matter. Not that you have to worry about her; she can get herself out. If you would be so kind as to open the door, we can rescue the dog and save the day.*"

Led by Rex, who was bounding along excitedly next to his human's right leg, Albert arrived at Mike's side.

The two men exchanged a glance and Mike asked, "You got any idea what it is that they're trying to tell us?"

Rex barked loudly at his human. "*Old man, I know you've learned to trust me, and I ask you to extend that faith another time. You won't be able to hear it, and I know you can't smell it, but there is a dog trapped inside here somewhere. He's been drugged, and people have been looking for him all day. I've done all the legwork ...*" he stopped to amend what he had just said, giving credit because it was due. "*Sorry, the three of us have done the legwork,"* he got nods of acknowledgement from Buster and Lila. *"Now I need you to do the one thing that I cannot do and open that door."*

"Excuse me?" Amber's indignant voice echoed out from inside the room. *"Where would you three idiot dogs be without the cat? Are you forgetting that I led you here? None of you had any idea who was behind this, and you would never have found the little dog were it not for me."*

"Goodness me," said Mike. *"Is that a cat I just heard?"*

Albert had heard it too of course. Bending at the waist, he placed his hands on his knees to keep himself steady as he came down closer to Rex's height.

"Is that it, boy? Is there a trapped cat inside that room? Is that what you're trying to tell me?"

Rex turned his head to look at his companions.

"How is it that humans can be so inventive and yet so utterly, hopelessly dumb?"

Lila replied, *"Just wag your tail, and let them get on with it. That's my motto."*

So Rex did just that, spinning on the spot for added emphasis when the two humans decided they were going to try to open the door.

Amber had already had enough of the dark, damp room, and the dopey, drugged dog. She was going back through the hole to see what was going on and to give the dogs a good piece of her mind since they were attempting to take all the credit for solving the mystery.

Closest to the missing brick, Buster spotted her wiggling to get back out and hastily hissed, "*Stay inside! The humans think they're coming to rescue you.*"

Amber spat, "*Get out of my way, you fat oaf!*"

"You better hurry, Mike," encouraged Albert. "It sounds like that cat is in some distress."

"*Distress?*" Amber repeated. "*You're damned skippy I'm in distress. I'm working with dogs. That's how low my life has sunk.*"

With Amber refusing to listen, and the danger that the humans would see her coming out of the hole and leave the door as it was, Buster backed up and blocked off the cat's escape route.

He was rewarded just a moment later when Amber sunk five claws into his derriere.

The suppressed squeak of sound he made drew everyone's attention.

"*Everything all right?*" Lila enquired, eyeing the bulldog curiously.

Through gritted teeth, Buster managed to mumble, "*Just peachy.*"

Mike knew that what he ought to do was leave Albert and the dogs at the door while he went to the hotel's reception to fetch a person from the maintenance team. Someone would have a key. However, doing that was likely to put him in close proximity with Chief Inspector Quinn who would most definitely ask why one of his detective sergeants was still hanging around when he ought to be on duty somewhere. Not only that, since the only reason Mike could come up with for the Chief Inspector to have returned was to apprehend Albert Smith, getting caught helping the fugitive would create a lot of additional drama he would rather do without.

It was with that in mind, that he reached forward to try the lock. With a snort of laughter, he discovered it wasn't even locked.

A short corridor stretched into the darkness beyond. Darkness that was scared away a moment later when Mike reached up to flick a light switch.

Rex shoved past Mike's legs to get into the corridor, his nose working double time. Immediately on the right was another door and beyond it Ernie's scent was unmistakable.

That the same ladies heeled footprints from outside had left small dirt marks on the painted floor raised a question in Mike's head, though he wasn't sure what to make of it. It had been a bizarre day. Instead of arresting a man wanted in connection with terrorist activities, he was helping him to find his dog. Now that he had found the dog, he was helping the dog to rescue a cat.

The dog had his head up against the door, making it quite clear he wanted Mike to open it.

Just like the outer door, it wasn't locked, and the doorknob was wrenched from Mike's hand the moment he got it open. The German

Shepherd shunted it with his head, barrelling through the gap and widening it with his body as he slammed the door out of his way.

The dachshund and bulldog followed, all three dogs barking excitedly and laying on the floor to stare beneath the bottom shelf of a rack loaded with five-gallon drums.

"The cat is under there?" Mike asked, following the dogs.

"*No*," said Amber, pausing in the doorway beside Albert's feet. "*The cat is behind you.*"

Her appearance could have scuppered the rescue attempt, but it was clear that the dogs thought there was something of interest in the gap beneath the bottom shelf.

"If I find there's a bone down here, I'm going to be mightily disappointed," Mike groaned as he lowered himself to the floor.

However, once he was lying flat on the grimy concrete, he saw what it was that had the three dogs so excited.

"Ha!" the word burst from his lips. "I don't believe it!"

Albert found himself coming closer, curiosity demanding he find out what drew the exclamation from the police officer.

"What did you find?"

Mike had to shove the bulldog out of the way as he shuffled forward to reach under the shelf.

"Remember when I told you about what I was doing here today?"

Albert cast his mind back. He'd assumed that the police were there for him, and it was only now that he recalled that Mike said something about a missing child.

"It was a missing child wasn't it that turned out to be nothing of the sort."

Mike withdrew his arms and swivelled around so that he was sitting. In his hands was a small furry lump, and on his face was a triumphant grin.

"The bride's dog went missing. Chief Inspector Quinn went nuts when he found out the truth. I'm not sure if they deliberately misled the dispatcher, or if it was one of those Chinese whispers cases and the information was simply misunderstood. Either way, Ernie isn't a little boy, it's a champion Pomeranian dog."

Mike shuffled his arms around so that he was cradling the dog with one hand and able to scratch at his ears with the other. He wasn't getting a lot of response from it and held it up so that he could look at the dog's face.

"I might need to get this little fellow to a vet. He looks like he's had a stroke."

Albert waded through the dogs to get a better look for himself.

"Nah, he's just drugged." Albert had seen the tongue hanging from the mouth look on his own dog more than once after a visit to the vet for surgery or some such. "We should get him out of here though."

Albert gave Mike a hand up and the two men led the three dogs back out into the hotel gardens.

Looking over his shoulder, Mike asked, "Is it normal for a cat to be hanging around with three dogs?"

"*No, it jolly well isn't,*" Amber answered before anyone else could.

Albert thought about that for a moment, his eyebrows knitting together as he considered the clues he could see. Pinning Rex in place with his eyes, he asked, "Is the cat with you?"

Rex wagged his tail. "*Yes.*"

"*I am most certainly not,*" argued Amber.

Still carrying the Pomeranian, Mike asked, "What do you want to do now, Albert? The way I see it, you've got just a couple of choices."

Albert reached down to ruffle the fur between Rex's ears. Now that he had his dog back, he could theoretically leave the hotel and just keep going. The police were here for him though, and that changed things.

"I'm not going to bother running if that's what you're asking. I have my dignity."

It was as Mike had expected and he had a suggestion.

"If memory serves, the wedding ceremony is due to take place any moment." Mike shot his cuff to confirm it was just after three o'clock in the afternoon. "This little fellow is supposed to be the bride's ring bearer. I think you should deliver him to the marquee, and I will seek out Chief Inspector Quinn."

Albert chewed on his top lip for a moment, trying to figure out what the Detective Sergeant was saying.

"What are you suggesting?"

"I had wanted to help you escape, Albert. I hope you believe that. However, now that Chief Inspector Quinn is here, the only thing I will achieve is the end of my career and it will make no difference to whether they arrest you or not. Instead, I propose to admit that I have been in your company for the last few hours, and that you surrendered to my custody. Chief Inspector Quinn will want to know why I didn't radio in immediately, and I will advise that I was employing your dog to help me find the bride's missing dog."

Albert's face was incredulous when he asked, "Do you think he'll go for that?"

Mike chuckled. "Not for a moment. However, he won't be able to prove otherwise. If you are as innocent as you say you are, you will be out of custody within just a couple of days, and with your permission I think I might like to take some time off to assist with your investigation. I can only do that if Quinn isn't trying to end my career. So, when he questions you about me, you'll need to corroborate my story."

Albert nodded his understanding. "I can do that. You'd better hand me the dog."

Mike handed Ernie the champion Pomeranian to Albert and the two men shook hands.

Starting to back away, Mike said, "I'll bring Quinn to the service. He'll be forced to tread carefully and quietly there and will see that we were telling the truth about finding the little dog."

It was a sound plan, and it was the only one they had.

Albert watched Mike hurry across the hotel's immaculate lawn, heading for the front of the building, then turned his attention towards the giant white marquee.

Nearing it, he could hear a string quartet playing and in the very next breath, they stopped and restarted with a far more familiar tune: the Wedding March.

Albert swore - the ceremony was already starting!

Here Comes The Bride

"Auntie, have you noticed that Denise Moscovitch's boyfriend isn't here?"

The ceremony was underway and holding her father's arm, the bride was advancing down the centrally set aisle toward the groom and best man at the front. I could feel my tension beginning to seep away. I had stationed myself in the back row and had Mindy to my right and Vince to my left.

Against all odds, and despite the bride's little dog still being missing, the wedding was going ahead. Now my niece was asking questions and once again my heart filled with doubt.

"You're right," I agreed, my eyes zipping through the congregation to confirm that he was nowhere in sight. I knew precisely where he was supposed to be: at the end of aisle three, ready to accompany the maid of honour after the ceremony had finished and everyone was filing outside for photographs. It brought to mind how disconnected he had seemed all day long, and how unbothered he had been earlier about his girlfriend's obvious distress.

Did I have a new suspect? Was he somewhere checking on Ernie?

Talking mostly to myself I said, "I wonder where he could be."

"Beats me," whispered Mindy. "Maybe he's wherever it is that Philippe got to."

"Oh, look," I pointed across the marquee to where Hudson had just snuck in and was trying to surreptitiously make his way to his appointed seat.

Denise shot him a look as the bridal party passed where he was supposed to be sitting.

"Ooh, she does not look pleased," murmured Mindy, just a little bit too loud. She caught a glare from the woman in front who clearly thought we ought to be silent during the ceremony.

I certainly wasn't going to argue because she was right.

Movement caught my eye as Philippe snuck in next to Mindy.

"Where have you been?" she hissed at him, drawing another glare from the woman in the next row.

There were beads of sweat on Philippe's brow and his hair was less than its usual perfection.

"I had important stuff to deal with," he whispered from the side of his mouth. "I'll tell you about it after the ceremony."

I wanted to know what it was that had kept him so busy and unable to help us for the last forty minutes. This, though, was not the time to grill him on the subject.

At the front of the gathering, Donna was being swapped from her father's arm to Damien's and the pastor was addressing the congregation.

Strategy Session

R ex narrowed his eyes at the parade of dogs standing outside the entrance to the marquee. Huffing out a breath he paused.

Carrying the Pomeranian with both hands and trusting Rex to stay at heel, Albert went a farther two paces before he realised he was by himself. Twisting around to see what had happened to them, he found the three dogs looking at the marquee where a row of large hounds were tied to the frame outside.

"Do you reckon they're there to stop us getting in?" Rex asked his companions.

Lila growled, *"Almost certainly. That Cerberus has got a lot to answer for. He's such a class snob."*

Buster twisted his neck left and right again, causing it to click in both directions. Dropping his voice to a husky rasp, he announced, *"Then I guess it's Devil Dog time. Are you ready Cherry Bomb?"*

Lila barked, *"I was born ready!"*

"How about you, Destructo Dog?" Buster tried out yet another name, wishing the German Shepherd would get on board.

Ignoring the silliness, Rex said, *"I don't think a straight attack is going to do it, guys. They might be tethered to the frame, but there's six of them, and they're all bigger than me. Even if we get by them, we then have to deal with the dogs inside who will know we are coming."*

"We can make it," insisted Devil Dog. *"I admit, it would help if my human would get me the side mounted rocket launchers I've been asking for, but the three of us can overcome any odds if we choose to."*

Acknowledging that arguing was almost certainly senseless, Rex chose another strategy.

"You're forgetting that their target is Ernie. That means they're going to go for my human, and I can't risk that."

"Dogs, what is going on?" Albert demanded to know. "I need to get this little one into that marquee. If you're not coming, then I'll go by myself. I'm not letting you out of my sight though, Rex. So you are going on the lead." It would be a juggle managing the dozy Pomeranian in one hand, and controlling Rex on his lead in the other, but Albert saw no choice. He'd spent a good chunk of the day trying to find his dog. There was no chance he was letting him out of his sight now.

Seeing his lead appear, Rex danced out of the way. To Buster and Lila, he barked, "*We need a plan! Fast!*"

Amber stretched out her front paws, arched her back and then stretched out her back legs one at a time as she limbered up.

"*Dogs, this really is very simple. If you want to walk into the marquee, all you need to do is get rid of the dogs that are in your way.*"

Staying just out of Albert's reach, Rex shot back, "*Oh, yeah? And how do we do that?*"

"*You get a superior creature involved. A cat.*" Amber walked two paces to get in front of Buster and whacked him on the nose with a paw. "*Hey, dog! Pay attention! I'm going to distract Cerberus and all his slobbering idiot friends. They are going to chase me, and I will require rescuing. If you do not promptly rescue me, I will make your life a living hell.*"

Rubbing at his nose, Buster said, "*Okay, psycho cat. I'm fairly sure you could have just asked instead of whacking me in the face.*"

Walking away, Amber called over her shoulder, "*Now what would be the fun in that?*"

STAMPEDE!

S tanding next to me, Mindy jumped at the sudden explosion of barking coming from just a few feet behind us and said a word that ought not to be repeated in church.

Vince craned his head around. "What on earth has got into them?" The noise coming from outside was already drowning out what the pastor was trying to say.

I had no idea, but all the other dogs - the ones whose owners believed could be trusted to sit quietly during the ceremony, were now on their feet and twisting around to look.

The barking outside was growing in volume, getting louder and louder when suddenly it seemed to swing in our direction. Something whipped under the edge of the marquee, a blur of something cream that was moving fast and close to the ground.

Vince nudged me and pointed a finger. "Hey, wasn't that ..."

I jabbed a sharp elbow into his ribs, silencing him before he could name my cat. It had taken my brain a moment to register that was what I had seen and everyone else was seeing it too.

There was no time for anyone to react, for there were a lot of things happening at once.

To begin with, the dogs tethered outside were trying to follow the cat. Allow me to amend that. They *were* following the cat and that was a problem because they were still tethered to the uprights supporting that end of the marquee.

The whole structure was trying to go with them, and with a squeal of fright, I realised the part of the marquee that I was in was about to collapse.

Amber had shot through the marquee and vanished from sight. My guess was that she had escaped out the front, but what she left in her wake was absolute bedlam. The forty or so dogs, who until a few seconds ago had been sitting or lying obediently next to their owners, were now bucking and fighting and trying to give chase.

In fact, most of them were giving chase, and those who were still trying to get free, were making a lot of noise in the process.

I heard someone yell and curse when their dog elected to bite them.

Donna was screaming. Her mother was screaming. The pastor was employing language I didn't think members of the clergy were permitted to even know, and as the rear end of the marquee folded behind me, and the back six rows began trampling those in front of them to escape, a stampede of furious dogs made a hole in the other end of the canvas structure.

REUNITED

Albert Smith believed he'd seen a lot of strange things in his life. Several decades as a police detective ensured that was true, but some of the weirdest events had come in the last few months. His dog, Rex Harrison, named by the police handlers who trained him, had been much like any other dog when they lived at home. He would go for a walk, he would come home, he would bark at the squirrels and cats in their garden, and he would count down the hours until it was dinner time.

However, when Albert chose to set off on a culinary tour around the British Isles, the dog had started to change. To be fair, everything had changed, and everywhere they went they seemed to run into yet another mystery. Somewhere in all the chaos, while Albert was trying to solve whatever crime he'd been presented with, Rex had stopped being a lazy house dog content to sleep the days away, and had become ... what?

Albert wasn't sure what term to employ. He'd watched as Rex came to his rescue on more than one occasion and at times it seemed as if the German Shepherd was attempting to assist him in his investigation. It was ridiculous, and Albert wasn't going to voice his thoughts to anyone, not even his children, who would probably send him for a CT scan. However, he could not shift the feeling that Rex understood exactly what was going on and what each situation required.

Standing outside the marquee, Albert had not been able to move fast enough to stop the cat whizzing toward the line of dogs. They reacted as if absolutely dumbfounded until the cat whipped between them and ran straight under the marquee's canvas edge.

Then Rex had taken off, the bulldog and dachshund sprinting after him as they went around the marquee and vanished from sight.

Speaking to the Pomeranian, who at least appeared to be awake now, Albert asked, "Do you know what's going on? I'm sure I don't."

Unable to stop it from happening, Albert had to watch as the six large hounds secured to the marquee's uprights at this end dove underneath the canvas and folded the legs in. The angle allowed their leads to slip free and the dogs vanished before they could pull the structure completely to the floor.

Screams and general noises of distress coming from inside the marquee, only fell quiet when the barking dwindled into the distance.

The marquee hadn't collapsed, though Albert thought that it might, and a few seconds after it settled into a new, rather drunken, position some of the people inside arrived to fight the uprights back to where they should be.

Strolling through the entrance, with Ernie the champion Pomeranian in his hands, Albert smiled at the faces staring back at him.

The back rows of the marquee had been evacuated. Clearly there had been a hurry to get away from the collapsing structure as most of the chairs were overturned. People were returning to them now, but they were also stopping to stare at the old man carrying the bride's dog.

Albert spotted a young woman he'd seen before. She was wearing a summery dress now and a fascinator in her hair, but it was the same girl he'd seen early this morning with the bulldog who was now accompanying Rex in whatever adventure the dogs were having.

She nudged the woman next to her, drawing her attention to the dog in Albert's arms.

The older woman - Albert placed her somewhere in her fifties, looked about to say something when a cry from the front of the congregation filled the air.

"Ernie!"

Albert looked around to find a young woman in a white dress running for him. Her hands had hold of her dress, lifting the skirt so she wouldn't trip. That he was looking at the bride required no explanation.

"Ernie!" she yelled again, and as she drew near, the little dog turned its head and gave a rather weak wag of his tail.

Albert tried to say something, intending to hand the dog over and explain where he found it, but the bride ripped Ernie from his grasp, and levelled an accusing glare at him.

"Who are you?" she demanded to know. "Why did you take my dog?"

Unexpectedly, Albert found himself surrounded by angry faces. The bride's question was being repeated by other people, and a hulking man that Albert took to be the bride's father, was advancing upon him with a menacing look dominating his features.

A shout of, "Somebody call the police!" just as the crowd was pressing in around him, was answered by a voice from the back of the marquee.

"There's no need, thank you. The police are already here."

THe wronG Tree

Amber doubted she had ever run faster in her life. Streaking across the lawn, she headed for a large Scots pine tree. It was one of a line of such trees which she had spotted prior to announcing her intention to save the day.

The pack of rabid dogs was gaining on her, and unlike earlier when they had been chasing her just because it was a game, now they intended to genuinely hurt her if the threats being aimed at her tail were anything to go by.

Nevertheless, and feeling really quite superior, Amber reached the tree several yards ahead of the nearest dog and proceeded to quickly scale it. This was the most dangerous part of her plan; the one bit where she could easily find herself getting torn to shreds if she didn't get high enough in time.

Thankful that there were no greyhounds in the chasing pack, Amber was still relieved when she spotted Rex tripping a rather speedy German Pointer.

She climbed a few more feet before deciding she was out of reach and got to test how high she needed to be when the first dogs arrived and tried to run up the tree to get to her.

Breathing a sigh of relief when they fell short, she clawed her way up another couple of feet to gain one of the lower branches. More and more dogs were gathering beneath her, all of them barking and snarling, their threats of unspeakable violence enough to make her blood chill.

Resting for a moment, Amber waited until she had her breath back, then climbed a little further into the tree so the greenery would hide her. Once she could no longer see the dogs and felt convinced the reverse was also true, she picked a branch that looked to have enough stretch and calmly sauntered along it - it wouldn't do to look flustered when she rejoined Buster.

Crossing into another tree, she made her way to the trunk and looked for a branch that would carry her to the next tree in line. Several trees later, she started her descent.

Because they knew to look for her, Rex, Lila, and Buster were at the base of the tree when she reached the ground, and she was pleased to hear their compliments.

It started with Buster. *"Amber, I have to tell you, that was really quite something."*

"Yeah," agreed Lila, *"I never would have thought a cat would do something like that. To help dogs, I mean. It's just not what cats do."*

"It was very brave," remarked Rex.

"It was, wasn't it?" Amber wasn't going to admit that she'd been terrified. Halfway to the tree, she feared the dogs were going to run her down. Now she was having to pretend that her body wasn't shaking from the adrenalin leaving it. Acting with her usual indifference, she lifted a paw to begin preening – her fur required straightening. However, it stopped halfway to her mouth when her eyes caught sight of the baying pack of dogs.

Humans from the marquee were heading for them, shouting and raging at the destruction their pedigree pets had wrought, and a laugh burst from Amber's lips.

Surprised by it, her canine companions all turned their heads to see where she was looking. A shared glance between Rex, Lila, and Buster found its way back to Amber who was still sniggering to herself.

Finding the dogs' questioning faces staring down at her, she wrestled her amusement under control. *"Don't you see?"* Amber asked, barely able to get the words out. *"They're barking up the wrong tree!"*

WHODUNIT?

I'd been forced to wait to approach Ernie's rescuer as the congregation had pressed in tight around him and were only now dissipating with DS Mike Atwell's encouragement.

We were right at the start of the ceremony and needed to get it back under way as quickly as possible – delays now would have a knock-on effect on the food and everything else. A bunch of guests were still outside trying to round up their dogs, and I had Justin, Philippe, and Mindy out there to lend a hand.

Donna was bawling her eyes out again, though this time it was tears of happiness as she hugged her little dog. Her makeup could be touched up before we started taking photographs.

I had questions for Mr Smith – I'd overheard him saying his name - but was still waiting to pose them because he was currently getting his arm pumped by the groom. Damien expressed his thanks before moving away, but there were at least half a dozen other people talking to Mr Smith including DS Mike Atwell who appeared behind Albert to whisper something.

He needed to speak more quietly, because I heard him say, "Chief Inspector Quinn had already departed before I got to reception. It would seem he was here to investigate another false report of a missing person. You are in the clear, old boy. I think perhaps we should avoid giving people your first name just in case they've been watching the local news."

I wasn't sure what that meant, but catching Mike's eye, I fired my question at him.

"Where was Ernie?"

The answer came not from Mike or the mysterious Mr Smith, but from a position close to my feet.

"*He was in a storeroom under the hotel,*" said Buster.

"In a storeroom?" I responded without thinking.

"*It was grimy and filled with cobwebs,*" complained Amber, startling me when she appeared by Buster's side. "*I had to go inside and locate the daft Pomeranian.*"

That Amber and Buster appeared to be working together was startling enough, but I had no time to question it for my comment had stolen the words from both men, who looked at me, then each other, and then me again.

"How did you know that?" asked Mr Smith.

With my cheeks burning, I stuttered, "Um, lucky guess." Now that I had his attention, I thrust out my hand. "Hello. I'm Felicity. I'm the wedding planner."

The elderly man had a confident grip when he shook my hand and met my eyes with an unwavering gaze.

"Al ..."

He was cut off by Mike Atwell kicking his foot.

"... fred," Mr Smith concluded. "Alfred Smith."

Buster nudged my leg. "*Rex says the culprit is in here somewhere. Her stink is all over Ernie. He and Cherry Bomb are trying to find the right person now.*"

"*Why are you not picking me up, Felicity?*" demanded Amber. "*I've been chased by dogs twice and I had to climb into a dirty hole and the whole day has been just the worst and these awful humans are not minding their feet and someone is going to step on my tail. Pick me up right now!*"

To shut her up as much as anything, I scooped Amber into my arms. When Mindy returned, I would ask my niece to take her back to my room – I would find out how she got out later, but Mike and Mr Smith were talking to me, asking questions, and trying to explain about how they found the missing Pomeranian and I couldn't keep up with the multiple conversations. Uttering a curse word under my breath, I was about to drop into a crouch to talk to Buster when the German Shepherd and miniature dachshund reappeared next to him.

Buster barked, "*They've found her!*"

I gasped, looking around the marquee as if there was going to be a big arrow hanging in the air to identify the guilty party.

Mr Smith spoke to the German Shepherd, "What's going on, Rex?" he produced a lead which he connected to the German Shepherd's collar thus removing any ambiguity over whose dog he was.

"He's yours?" I asked, nevertheless.

With a nod, Mr Smith said, "Yes. The bulldog is yours? I saw him with a young woman. Your daughter?"

"My niece."

Though I was doing my best to focus on speaking to Mr Smith, I couldn't help overhearing the conversation between the animals. Not that I was getting all of it, just what Buster and Amber were saying.

"*Which one is it, Rex?*"

I strained my hearing for no good reason – I wasn't going to 'hear' the German Shepherd's answer.

"*You'll have to show me,*" Buster started moving forward, but Rex was tethered to his owner, Mr Smith. Looking up at me, Buster said, "*Can you get Rex's human to follow me?*"

I bit my lip, "Um."

Mike Atwell and Mr. Smith were both looking my way, curious expressions on their faces as they wondered what it was I was doing. How was I supposed to explain that the dogs knew who it was that had taken Ernie? I wasn't going to come out and reveal my ability, so I had to come up with something else.

I lied.

"I believe I have figured out who's behind all of today's shenanigans," I whispered a prayer, begging for forgiveness. "Can you come with me please?" I addressed the request to the detective sergeant, that feeling more natural, but hoping that Alfred would come with me anyway.

Thankfully he did, allowing Rex to lead the way alongside Buster as we closed in on the wedding saboteur.

It was to my great surprise that we were led directly to the Moscovitch's. The bride's parents, her bridesmaids and her older sister, Denise, were gathered around Donna who was still cuddling Ernie.

Looking up as she saw me approaching, Donna said, "What a day this has been." Turning her attention to Mr. Smith, she passed Ernie to her sister and came forward to wrap her arms around the man who had returned her pet.

Alfred looked a little surprised by her affectionate act and was very careful to place just one hand on her waist.

"I can never thank you enough, Mr Smith. You don't know what this little doggie means to me."

While that was going on, Buster, Rex, and Lila had all pointed out who was behind Ernie's disappearance.

There was no ambiguity in their accusation, and they were steadfast in their certainty.

"*She smells of the storeroom where we found Ernie*," Buster relayed what Rex was saying, "*and her shoes smell of the soil outside the storeroom door. She also smells of Ernie, of course, which is a clever cover because she's holding him right now.*"

As evidence goes, it was nothing at all, and I certainly couldn't use it - how was I to explain that I could smell the guilt on her?

Nevertheless, I could see that it was true, and I was gawping at Denise with my mouth hanging open.

"Is there something the matter, Felicity?" Denise asked, wanting to know why I was staring at her.

"It was you," I blurted without thinking.

Denise responded with an obvious question, "What was me?"

"Her?" Mike questioned. "The bride's sister was behind it all?"

Denise's cheeks flushed - she knew she was guilty, but her mother and her sister were reacting in horror.

"What!" shrieked Mrs Moscovitch. "What are you saying Mrs Philips? Denise had nothing to do with Ernie's disappearance or anything else that has happened today. How could you think such a thing?"

Donna was eyeing me with suspicion. "Yeah. Denise has been by my side all day. And she got poisoned just like the other girls."

Denise was going to deny it, which came as no surprise, and now I had everyone in the bride's wedding party looking my way as they waited for me to expand on my statement.

My feet were rooted to the spot. I'm the wedding planner. I'm THE wedding planner, and what I do not do is go around accusing my clients of ... anything. How on earth could I back out of this conversation now?

My mouth had gone dry, and I was searching for something to say, when I saw Philippe re-entering the ruined back end of the marquee. There were some men there - wedding guests in suits - attempting to fix the canvas back into place, but it wasn't them or Philippe who I was looking at, but the man who came in next to Philippe.

I blinked, and absentmindedly touched a little itch by my left ear as the answers aligned in my head.

"Your boyfriend is gay," I stated, my eyes locked on Denise's. "Is he even your boyfriend?"

Again, it was Mrs Moscovitch who answered. "What? What on earth are you talking about, Mrs Philips?"

I didn't look her way, which was probably rather rude, and it was simply because Denise was looking so wretchedly guilty.

I pressed on, "You're the one who poisoned the bridesmaids, aren't you? You were never really sick. When we couldn't find you, were you checking on Ernie?"

"*She was,*" said Amber, twitching her tail. I was using one arm to hold her against my chest. "*I saw her in the gardens. That's how I was able to lead the dogs to find Ernie.*"

This time Donna came to her sister's defence. "But she was ill. You said so yourself."

I nodded, accepting the point she made, but argued, "She certainly appeared to be ill, I'll give you that. But the three bridesmaids were all treated by a doctor, that is how they made their recovery. Denise did not receive the treatment, did you, Denise?"

Denise said nothing, and now the eyes of the group were beginning to swing her way. Why wasn't she defending herself?

"I'm sure there were a lot of people who had access to your sister's phone today; there were lots of you in and out of the bridal suite, but who among you could have easily taken Ernie without him making a fuss? And who knew Donna's past so well that they could have contacted an ex-boyfriend who would turn up here today to cause upset?"

The colour had drained from Denise's face, and she was still to say anything - the lack of denial proof enough so far as I was concerned.

It wasn't enough for her family though.

Mrs Moscovitch turned on me. "How dare you? How dare you level accusations at my daughter? Where is your proof?"

Denise finally broke her silence, "Oh, stop it, mother," she cried, tears falling from her eyes as the focus swung back towards her and she backed away under the unwelcome pressure. "Of course it was me."

Her statement silenced everyone.

But not for long.

The first to react was Juniper. "You poisoned me, you insane cow!" To get to Denise she had to come around Donna and Mrs Moscovitch, and that was precisely what she was trying to do, both hands outstretched as if she intended to throttle the maid of honour.

Her reaction sparked Ellie and Christy into action.

"You made me mess my knickers!" yelled Ellie as she too made a beeline for the bride's sister.

Moving swiftly, Detective Sergeant Mike Atwell blocked their path, placing his body between the three murderous bridesmaids and the bride's sister.

Mrs Moscovitch looked faint. "Why, Denise? Why would you do that? Why would you do any of it?"

Denise's face had crumpled, and she looked utterly miserable as she tried to provide an answer that might explain her actions.

Surprising myself, I came to her rescue. I knew precisely why she had done it and I knew only too well the emotions behind it because I had seen them displayed earlier today. The circumstances would be completely different, yet the result was exactly the same. This was Ginny and me all over again.

My words were soft and gentle when I explained, "Because you favour her younger sister."

Mrs Moscovitch reacted as if slapped and Mr Moscovitch, even though he wasn't saying anything, looked just as surprised by my statement.

"No, I do not," argued Denise's mother.

Donna, looking glum, reached out a hand to take her older sister's, and said, "Yes you do, Mum. You always have."

The girls' parents both looked aghast and could offer no argument as they watched the bride embrace her older sister. Denise was shaking, her body suffering an enormous release of emotion, and she sobbed into her sister's shoulder.

With her broken voice, Denise croaked, "I didn't hurt Ernie. I just slipped him one of his travel pills and tucked him away safe. He was never in any danger."

Donna's reply was shocking. "You should have said something." There was no anger, no bitter recrimination. Where others might have been screaming and lashing out, the bride was acting as if she should be blamed for Denise's actions.

When someone tapped my arm, I turned to find Mike Atwell.

"I don't think there's any need for me to stay here; there's nothing criminal to investigate. I'm going to leave now, Felicity. Mr Smith and I have other tasks to which we must attend."

I turned so that I was facing him, and shuffled Amber to free my right hand. I shook with Mike first and then offered my hand to Alfred. There was something familiar about his face, I had decided. I couldn't figure out what it was, but expected it would come to me later.

"Thank you, both. Returning Ernie has probably saved this wedding."

Mike dipped his head in acknowledgement and tapped a hand to his forehead in a sort of salute.

"All in a day's work, Madam."

Alfred tugged at his dog's lead, encouraging him to start moving. "Come along, Rex. It's time for us to hit the road."

He said it in such a way that made me think he was taking a trip and it was clear that he wanted to get going. However, Rex had other ideas.

The fur running down the German Shepherd's spine was standing on end, and his body looked poised for action. To his right, Buster was doing the exact same thing, and to Rex's left, the dachshund had begun to growl.

They were all staring in the same direction, at the groom's champion Doberman I discovered when I tracked their eyes to see what they were looking at.

DOGS

Buster planted his paws and tensed the muscles in his back legs as he got ready. Cerberus had returned, and he was already baring his teeth at the three dogs who had thwarted his plans.

"What is that ridiculous toy dog doing back here?" growled the Doberman.

"Cerberus, behave," commanded his human, paying little attention to what his dog was doing as he began talking to the bride and her family. Above the dogs' heads, the humans were explaining what the groom had missed.

Rex narrowed his eyes. It wasn't so much that he wanted to fight the Doberman, but he was still smarting from being forced to walk away earlier and for the first time the muscular, prize-winning dog was without his bodyguards.

Whatever happened, Rex wasn't about to take any more of the Doberman's nonsense.

Snarling, Rex said, "*We tracked Ernie down and rescued him, just like we said we were going to.*"

"*Yeah,*" echoed Lila. "*And there's nothing you can do about it. We win, you lose, Cerberus, you big loser.*"

Saliva dripped from the Doberman's jowls as he peeled back his lips to snarl at the smaller dog.

"*Loser? I was second reserve for best in show! You were merely best in breed. You are beneath me, tiny dog. Just like that ridiculous toy.*"

Buster wanted to teach the arrogant dog a lesson, but just as he twitched his body at the start of his charge, a hand looped through his collar.

He yelped in surprise, as he was born aloft to find Mindy was the one preventing his attack.

"*No!*" he whined. "*I need to give the Doberman a sound beating.*"

Rex attempted to surge forward, but Albert knew his dog only too well, and had already braced to prevent any such action.

Rex twisted and fought against his restraint even as the Doberman's laughter filled his ears.

Cerberus stared down at the tiny dachshund.

"*I guess that just leaves you,*" he growled at Lila, his voice dripping with amusement.

The banshee cry the miniature dachshund made as she exploded into action was loud enough to capture the attention of every dog and human in the marquee.

"*I'm going to kill you!*" Lila screamed at the top of her lungs, surging across the carpeted floor in a move so unexpected that it caught the Doberman completely by surprise.

Wriggling in Mindy's arms, Buster stopped his struggles to watch his latest superhero sidekick, and cheered, "*Yeah! Go Cherry Bomb, go!*"

Unable to get out of the way quickly enough, and too stunned to launch a defensive counter strike that might deflect the sausage dog's attack, Cerberus did nothing until Lila ran between his front paws and leapt into the air.

She knew precisely what she was aiming for - they were hanging from the larger dog's undercarriage, a tempting soft target that she was able to sink her teeth into.

The look of shock on the Doberman's face was one that would stay with Rex and Buster for the rest of their lives.

Though her mouth was clamped tightly shut, Lila trumpeted, "*You got cherry bombed!*"

Unable to stop himself, Buster offered an apology to Mindy, and kicked out with his back legs. momentarily hanging in free air, he had to twist himself around to get his paws back beneath his body before he hit the ground.

Instantly sprinting, he bellowed, *"Dun, dun, DAH! It's Devil Dog time!"* as he went to join the fight.

Cerberus, yelping uncontrollably, and unable to do anything about the tiny black and tan dog hanging from his tenderest parts, did the only thing his brain could come up with: he ran.

Rex stared up at his human. *"Sorry. But I have to. It's a dog thing,"* he explained. In a manoeuvre he kept reserved for special occasions, Rex flattened his ears to his head, closed his mouth, and threw his body weight backwards. His head popped free of the collar around his neck, and just like Buster, he chased after the Doberman.

Barking loudly so everyone would hear, just as he caught up with Buster, Rex proudly declared in an exaggerated voice, *"Beware villains, Rexanator is here!"*

A grin spread across Buster's face, and he tipped his head back to howl, *"Yeah! That's the best superhero name yet!"*

Back in the marquee, a sea of humans watched the four dogs vanish into the distance.

Not that anybody other than Felicity heard her, but Amber captured the moment perfectly with a single word, *"Dogs."*

THE AFTER DINNER SPEECHES

"Could I fetch you a glass of something, Auntie?" asked Mindy.

I turned my head away from watching the after-dinner speeches.

"Thank you, but no. Vince is fetching me a gin and tonic."

"Is he now?" Mindy replied with an annoying wink, as she waltzed off to speak with Philippe.

My second assistant was in hot water and working hard to impress me. As the truth about everything came out, we discovered that Denise's supposed boyfriend was in fact a high price escort who she had hired to accompany her for the day. She didn't want to be seen as the sad spinster left on the shelf while her prettier, younger sister married the man of her dreams.

That Hudson was gay was a fact Denise had not known, but also didn't care about. He was only there to make her look good, a task he singularly failed at by generally neglecting to pay her any attention at all. Instead, he'd chosen to exchange numbers with Philippe, then exchange messages, and that led to ... well, I'm sure I don't need to explain what they were up to when they both went missing together.

Philippe and I were going to have a very one-sided conversation on Monday morning. For now, I was content to let him run around doing all that he could to make me believe that he really wanted his job.

Vince returned with my beverage, a large balloon glass with at least a double shot of Hendricks gin in it. I took a sip and then took another. I had to drive home tonight, but I wouldn't be behind the wheel for several hours yet.

After we had rounded up Rex and Buster and the little dachshund who I finally learned was called Lila, Mike and the mysterious Mr Smith departed. I had Mindy take Buster and Amber back to my room, and with Justin by my side, we had ushered the wedding guests back to their seats.

The ceremony took place without another hitch and the pastor made light of the stampeding dogs and exciting situations to entertain the congregation. It lightened the mood, which was generally confused about quite what was happening between the bride, her bridesmaids, her parents, and the maid of honour.

The groom's champion Doberman was demoted once again from the role of ring bearer, the little Pomeranian taking his place once he was alert enough to do so.

Of the Doberman there was no sign. I don't think he was injured; I saw where the dachshund bit him, but the groom seemed unconcerned that there was any damage. The dog's absence, in Buster's opinion, the last comment he made before Mindy led him away, was due to shame.

According to Buster, the Doberman had just lost his place as pack alpha, and the dogs were looking at Lila to take his place even though she wasn't a male dog.

It was all too confusing for me, and I suspected one had to be a dog to understand the politics involved.

Feeling the first tendrils of alcohol seeping into my blood stream, I did something unexpected and leaned into Vince. He was right there next to me as he had been, in spirit at least, pretty much all day.

We were going out for dinner on Tuesday to a restaurant of my choosing, and he seemed only too happy to be giving our relationship a second go. Or was it third?

As he tentatively put one arm around me, I decided it didn't really matter.

We were right at the back of the marquee where the wedding breakfast was taking place and from our vantage point tucked out of the way, we were watching the groom make his speech.

The only person left to talk was the father of the bride. With a jolt, I remembered the gun.

"You said you disabled that rifle, right?" I gabbled my words, pushing away from Vince again so I could turn round to look at his face.

I had just heard Damien hand over to Mr Moscovitch, and the father of the bride was rising from his chair.

Vince had an amused expression on his face that made no sense at all in the circumstances.

Hearing the round of applause that greeted Mr Moscovitch, I swung my head and eyes back around to see what was happening.

The father of the bride was reaching behind his chair, and it was with horror that I saw him lift the golf bag into sight. He was unzipping it to expose the weapon he had inside. Vince might have disabled it, but when it didn't work would Mr Moscovitch just produce a different weapon or elect to kill his intended target with his bare hands?

My blood froze in the next moment, as around the periphery of the marquee half a dozen men in their dark suits - the exact same men I'd seen meeting surreptitiously with Mr Moscovitch - stepped out from behind folds in the canvas.

They all had objects in their hands!

What was I witnessing?

Were they about to start shooting everyone? Was this about to become some kind of twisted wedding massacre? The man who looked like an undertaker was staring intently at Mr Moscovitch - waiting for a signal to start.

I sucked in a deep lungful of air to scream a warning.

Vince clamped his hand across my mouth before the sound could leave my body, and his other arm looped around my waist to stop me from ripping my way free.

"Shhhh. Just watch," he sniggered into my ear.

Two seconds had passed, and Mr Moscovitch now had the rifle in his hands. However, the presence of the ugly black weapon was nowhere near as surprising as the wedding guests' complete lack of response to it.

There was a man standing in front of them holding a deadly weapon, and none of them seemed even slightly bothered.

Imagine my enormous surprise when Mr Moscovitch reached into his trouser pocket and withdrew a microphone. It wasn't another gun I'd seen him putting in there at all. Then he began to sing.

Vince loosened his grip on me and took his hand away from my mouth.

The men in dark suits positioned at intervals around the outer edge of the marquee had lifted the objects they were holding, and I could see now that they were musical instruments.

Vince whispered to me, "I can't believe you didn't know."

I had no words to express the bewilderment I felt. It was as if the world had just been turned upside down.

Not only was Mr Moscovitch singing, he had the most beautiful operatic tenor voice. Not that he was singing opera, it sounded more like a pop song, and with a spasm I realised that I recognised it.

The bride's father was singing, '*Apple of my Eye*, by *The Criminals*'.

My jaw dropped open.

I had stopped paying any attention to popular music more than twenty-five years ago. I listened to it occasionally on my radio in the car, but apart from a few ultra-famous faces, I couldn't pick a pop star out of a crowd, and this was evidenced most clearly because I was staring right at one.

Mr Moscovitch looked like he was a criminal because that was his style. His costume, if you like, and the men positioned around the marquee were his band members. He was famous, and it also explained where his money came from.

How was it that I'd gone through all these meetings with his family, and this had never come up?

It even explained why he rarely spoke: he was protecting his voice.

As I listened to the lyrics, Vince placed a tender arm around me again.

"I apologise for not telling you the truth. You were so convinced that he was up to no good, it was simply too good of an opportunity to miss."

"You convinced Mindy to play along too, didn't you?"

Vince chuckled, his chest shaking against my back in a pleasant way.

"Yes. Your niece rather likes me."

He wasn't bragging, I already knew it was true. Vince was actually quite likeable when he wasn't being a total rogue. Unfortunately for me, the roguish side of him was present most of the time. I was going to have to have a chat with him about that.

"He's changed the lyrics," I remarked, realising that Mr Moscovitch had tailored his song so it was all about his daughter on her wedding day. "It's beautiful." I wiped a tear away from my right eye, unexpectedly caught up in the emotion of the moment.

My phone rang in my handbag. It was set to silent, but I could feel it vibrating against my hip.

I moved away from Vince and ducked out of the marquee to answer it. The number displayed on the screen was not one that I recognised, so it was my polished business response that the caller got.

"Felicity Philips, wedding planner to the stars. How may I help you?"

The voice that replied was one that sent a spike of ice directly through my heart.

"Mrs Philips, this is Edgar Whitechapel at the palace."

This was it. This was the call I had been waiting for. That the imminent announcement about who would be planning the next royal wedding had slipped my mind demonstrated more clearly than any-thing else just how crazy my day had been.

"Mrs Philips?" Edgar questioned when I failed to reply.

"Yes," I croaked, barely able to get the words out.

"Mrs Philips I'll get straight to the point. From the very start you were considered to be a top contender to plan Prince Marcus's wedding. However, in the light of recent events, the prince and his bride have chosen to employ a different wedding planner. The royal family wish to thank you for your application and wish you luck in your future business. Thank you. Good evening."

The line went dead, the dial tone replacing Edgar's voice to drone in my ear.

I felt numb. Had that really just happened? I don't like to think of myself as arrogant, and I wouldn't want to believe that I had an over bloated opinion of myself, but I knew I was the best person for the job.

The question of who had got the contract instead of me was answered in the next moment when movement caught my eye.

Standing on the patio outside the hotel bar, Primrose Green was hold-ing a glass of champagne. When she saw me looking her way, she lifted it in a salute to me.

She had known. I could see it now and it explained her absolute confidence in the bar and the surprise she didn't want to spoil. As the successful applicant she had been given advanced notice and had come here today so that she could gloat. It was written all over her face, but of course it was her. I had never really believed that I had a rival for the role other than her.

And Edgar had been clear about what it was that prevented me from being awarded the contract: my recent run of disastrous weddings.

I wanted to cry, but would not allow myself to indulge such an emotion. What was it that I would be crying about? Losing to a rival?

Tucking my phone away, I strode across the darkened hotel lawn to shake Primrose's hand. I would be generous in defeat and wish her every luck.

EPILOGUE:

Two days after the events at Champney's Resort and Spa Hotel, Detective Sergeant Mike Atwell found himself summoned to Chief Inspector Quinn's office.

There was nothing particularly unusual about this; there could have been any one of a number of reasons behind the chief inspector's request for a meeting, but walking through the station, Mike found himself feeling unexpectedly trepidatious.

He knocked on the outer door and waited until the chief inspector looked up and flipped his fingers to beckon he come inside.

"You wanted to see me, Sir?"

The chief inspector didn't answer straight away; he was busy with something on his computer and finished doing that, taking several seconds before he turned his attention Mike's way.

"Yes, DS Atwell. I rather think we need to have a conversation."

Mike lowered himself into a chair and waited for his boss to get to the point.

Swivelling the monitor of his computer so that Mike could see it, the chief inspector sat back in his chair and said nothing.

On the screen was a still picture that showed the wedding of Donna Moscovitch and Damien Ellis. Neither the bride nor groom were in the shot, however Mike was, and standing right next to him was Albert Smith.

Once he had given Detective Sergeant Atwell sufficient time to absorb what he was seeing, Chief Inspector Quinn asked, "Would you like to explain this? Would you care to find a reason why you were in the company of a man who I am trying to capture? A man who is wanted in connection with terrorist activities."

A smile creased Mike's face.

"Something amusing?" Chief Inspector Quinn asked, his tone changing to one of warning.

Turning his eyes away from the screen to look directly into his boss's eyes, Mike challenged him, "I don't think you believe that Albert Smith is involved in any terrorist activities. I don't believe that for one moment. I spoke to a few of the lads who were in Whitstable that night and they say that the old man did everything he could to warn you about what was about to happen. You're embarrassed that you didn't listen and now you're trying to cover it up by levelling the blame at an old man."

The Chief Inspector leaned forward in his chair, placing his forearms on his desk before he calmly replied, "How did he know that there was going to be an explosion? How did he know that there were explosives in the area? That old man has intimate knowledge, and he will surrender it to me so that my task force can arrest those responsible if indeed he is not involved. You prevented that from happening by willingly allowing him to escape your custody."

Feeling surprisingly buoyant even though he could feel his career as a police officer slipping away, Mike was grinning when he said, "He was never in my custody. I spoke to him, and his innocence was completely obvious. As is your incompetence, Chief Inspector."

Outside of the chief inspector's office, every cop in the station heard him roar.

"How dare you? You're done as a police officer! I'll see you hounded out of the service! I'll have your pension! I'll have your badge! You'll never work another day!"

Mike rose to his feet, took out his police identification, gave it a last look, and threw it in the chief inspector's face. It bounced off his nose before coming to rest on the desk between his balled fists.

"I think I'll save you the bother. I quit."

Clearly this was not what the chief inspector was expecting.

"Quit? You can't quit? You're a career police officer. You're too young to be unemployed."

"Oh, I already have another job offer, thank you for your concern."

"What? What job? What are you talking about?"

Mike didn't bother to reply, his thoughts were already elsewhere, and he could feel an enormous weight lifting off his shoulders now that he had gone through with something he'd been considering for several months.

"You know," he announced mostly to himself, "It's been really quite a while since I had a proper holiday. I went on a cruise not so long ago, but it wasn't really a vacation. I was working. I think perhaps I'll try that again. Only this time with a lot more relaxation included." Walking out the door, he remarked with a wink at his former boss, "I know just the lady to call about it."

The End

AUTHOR'S NOTES

H ello, Dear Reader,

As is so very often the case, I had no idea how long this book was going to be. At sixty thousand words it is probably ten thousand words longer than I anticipated. Not that I'm suggesting this is a problem; when I set out to write a book, my only aim is to do a good job of telling the tale I have locked inside my head.

During the process of crafting this story, a conversation with my wife lead to a relatively detailed mental plot for the next book. However, book six in this series will occur after Felicity has attended a wedding on board a cruise ship.

If you are one of those readers who voraciously devour everything as I release it, you will already know that Felicity and her niece are shortly to rendezvous with Patricia Fisher's cruise ship, the Aurelia, in Miami.

When I started publishing books five years ago, the concept of intertwining my series had not occurred to me. In fact, it was only after I'd finished writing the first series of Patricia Fisher books and had landed her back in her hometown close to where my Blue Moon series is set that it occurred to me to have the characters meet.

Everything that has followed, all the crossovers that have taken place, and are planned for the future, are due to a magical confluence of opportunity and ability.

In this book, I was able to bring Albert and Rex directly into contact with Felicity Philips and her pets. The chance to write Buster, Amber, and Rex together was just too good to miss. They will meet again at the end of Felicity's series, but I'm not going to tell you any more about that just yet.

Albert and Rex are on their way to Cornwall and are nearing the end of their first series of books. Fans of my old man and dog duo need not despair that their tale is coming to an end though, for I have two more series planned.

Detective Sergeant Mike Atwell is a character I created at the end of Patricia Fisher's first series of books. Needing a local police officer who would assist Patricia in solving her cases, I inadvertently created a character who was simply too interesting to leave alone when Patricia returned to sea.

He has already appeared in Felicity's first story and has popped up elsewhere in my books. My intention now is to give him his own spin-off series. At this time I have nothing more than an idea in my head and no time to write it. I have to finish at least one of my series before I start something new, but setting the foundations for it now, seems only prudent.

In this book I mentioned the Cornish seaside town of Looe. Pronounced 'loo' it is a destination I have visited many times in my life. Built long before anyone considered the concept of a motorised vehicle, most of these streets are far too narrow to allow a car which of course only adds to the quaintness.

Cornwall is one of my favourite counties in the United Kingdom, not that I can boast to have visited all or even half of them, but the blend of jagged coastline, remoteness, and romantic sweeping hills, draws me to it like nowhere else on earth. Indeed, it surprises me that I have only set one of my seventy plus titles to date in the nation's most south westerly county.

I look forward to returning soon with Albert and Rex. Perhaps at some point in the future I will write an entire series set in Cornwall and will happily decide that I need to perform weeks of research touring the hidden valleys and ancient villages.

It is very often the case that I finish my books late at night or even early in the morning, pushing to get to the end in a final flourish of words that takes far more hours than I had anticipated. I wrote ten thousand words yesterday hoping that I might get to the end of this story, but fatigue drove me to my bed so as I write this final note it is nearing noon on a Tuesday.

Outside the window of my log cabin at the bottom of my garden the sun is shining brightly. Butterflies and birds are flitting between the bushes and trees, and I have to say that I have one of the most wonderful places in the world in which to write. Not just because of the scenery, you understand, but because my wife and children are just a few yards away across the garden when I want to see them.

I measure my success by such privileges and know that I am rich indeed for them.

One item I feel I must clear up is the subject of the wedding breakfast. When I sent this book to my advance reading team, I receive a lot of questions regarding the serving of beef Wellington and lobster for breakfast. Wedding breakfast is the term give for the meal served immediately after the ceremony and traditionally is a three-course sit-down meal. It has nothing to do with cornflakes.

Now I'm going to close this book and invite you to scroll down a few pages, or indeed turn them if you are reading a physical copy, for you will find the next book in this series and indeed other series from which you might wish to select your future reading material.

Take care.

Steve Higgs.

WHaT'S NeXT FOr FeLICITY PHILIPS?

Something Stole, Something Blue

She should say no.She's not a detective after all.But how can she?When Felicity Philips receives a panicked call from an old friend, there simply isn't a way that she can turn him down.Edward, the jeweller to the crown, is in deep trouble and he cannot tell the police. His terrible truth must be kept secret.But what is his motivation for calling Felicity? Does he really believe she is the only one who can help? Or are his motivations more personal and dark than he is letting on?With her usual cast of supporting misfits, Felicity is going to see what she can do ...... but when she uncovers the truth, will she be able survive it?

SOMETHING STOLE SOMETHING BLUE
STEVE HIGGS

More Books By Steve Higgs

Blue Moon Investigations
Paranormal Nonsense
The Phantom of Barker Mill
Amanda Harper Paranormal Detective
The Klowns of Kent
Dead Pirates of Cawsand
In the Doodoo With Voodoo
The Witches of East Malling
Crop Circles, Cows and Crazy Aliens
Whispers in the Rigging
Bloodlust Blonde – a short story
Paws of the Yeti
Under a Blue Moon – A Paranormal
Detective Origin Story
Night Work
Lord Hale's Monster
The Herne Bay Howlers
Undead Incorporated
The Ghoul of Christmas Past
The Sandman
Jailhouse Golem
Shadow in the Mine

Felicity Philips Investigates
To Love and to Perish
Tying the Noose
Aisle Kill Him
A Dress to Die For

Patricia Fisher Cruise Mysteries
The Missing Sapphire of Zangrabar
The Kidnapped Bride
The Director's Cut
The Couple in Cabin 2124
Doctor Death
Murder on the Dancefloor
Mission for the Maharaja
A Sleuth and her Dachshund in Athens
The Maltese Parrot
No Place Like Home

Patricia Fisher Mystery Adventures
What Sam Knew
Solstice Goat
Recipe for Murder
A Banshee and a Bookshop
Diamonds, Dinner Jackets, and Death
Frozen Vengeance
Mug Shot
The Godmother
Murder is an Artform
Wonderful Weddings and Deadly
Divorces
Dangerous Creatures

Patricia Fisher: Ship's Detective Series
The Ship's Detective
Fitness Can Kill
Death by Pirates

Albert Smith Culinary Capers
Pork Pie Pandemonium
Bakewell Tart Bludgeoning
Stilton Slaughter
Bedfordshire Clanger Calamity
Death of a Yorkshire Pudding
Cumberland Sausage Shocker
Arbroath Smokie Slaying
Dundee Cake Dispatch
Lancashire Hotpot Peril
Blackpool Rock Bloodshed
Kent Coast Oyster Obliteration

Realm of False Gods
Untethered magic
Unleashed Magic
Early Shift
Damaged but Powerful
Demon Bound
Familiar Territory
The Armour of God
Live and Die by Magic
Terrible Secrets

ABOUT THE AUTHOR

At school, the author was mostly disinterested in every subject except creative writing, for which, at age ten, he won his first award. However, calling it his first award suggests that there have been more, which there have not. Accolades may come but, in the meantime, he is having a ball writing mystery stories and crime thrillers and claims to have more than a hundred books forming an unruly queue in his head as they clamour to get out. He lives in the south-east corner of England with a duo of lazy sausage dogs. Surrounded by rolling hills, brooding castles, and vineyards, he doubts he will ever leave, the beer is just too good.

www.ingramcontent.com/pod-product-compliance
Lightning Source LLC
Chambersburg PA
CBHW070544190726
48291CB00017B/2219